INVASION OF P9-AQA-249

It was hard to believe the same Julie who was always so quiet in school was seething with frustration at home. Sarah was also amazed that Julie continued to write so honestly when she knew Sarah would be reading her journal.

But as Sarah began to close the journal, she noticed something that she clearly wasn't supposed to see. At the bottom of the page were a few words Julie had written, then crossed out with another pen. Sarah stared at the page, trying to read what the other girl had written. Finally she made out the words: *It all ends Wednesday.*

18 Pine St.

The Diary

Written by
Stacie Johnson

Created by
WALTER DEAN MYERS

A Seth Godin Production

BANTAM BOOKS
NEW YORK · TORONTO · LONDON · SYDNEY · AUCKLAND

RL 5, age 10 and up

THE DIARY
A Bantam Book / June 1994

Thanks to Susan Korman, Amy Berkower, Fran Lebowitz, Marva Martin, Michael Cader, Megan O'Connor, José Arroyo, Julie Maner, Chris Angelilli, Karen Watts, Ellen Kenny, Helene and Lucy Wood.

18 Pine St. is a trademark of Seth Godin Productions, Inc.

ISBN 0-553-56563-X

Published simultaneously in the United States and Canada

Bantam Books are published by Bantam Books, a division of Bantam Doubleday Dell Publishing Group, Inc. Its trademark, consisting of the words "Bantam Books" and the portrayal of a rooster, is Registered in U.S. Patent and Trademark Office and in other countries. Marca Registrada. Bantam Books, 1540 Broadway, New York, New York 10036.

PRINTED IN THE UNITED STATES OF AMERICA

OPM 0 9 8 7 6 5 4 3 2 1

For Brooke

18 Pine St.

There is a card shop at 8 Pine St., and a shop that sells sewing supplies at 10 Pine that's only open in the afternoons and on Saturdays if it doesn't rain. For some reason that no one seems to know or care about, there is no 12, 14, or 16 Pine. The name of the pizzeria at 18 Pine St. was Antonio's before Mr. and Mrs. Harris took it over. Mr. Harris removed Antonio's sign and just put up a sign announcing the address. By the time he got around to thinking of a name for the place, everybody was calling it 18 Pine.

The Crew at 18 Pine St.

Sarah Gordon is the heart and soul of the group. Sarah's pretty, with a great smile and a warm, caring attitude that makes her a terrific friend. Sarah's the reason that everyone shows up at 18 Pine St.

Tasha Gordon, tall, sexy, and smart, is Sarah's cousin. Since her parents died four years ago, Tasha has moved from relative to relative. Now she's living with Sarah and her family—maybe for good.

Cindy Phillips is Sarah's best friend. Cindy is petite, with dark, radiant skin and a cute nose. She wears her black hair in braids. Cindy's been Sarah's neighbor and friend since she moved from Jamaica when she was three.

Kwame Brown's only a sophomore, but that doesn't stop him from being part of the crew. As the smartest kid in the group, he's the one Jennifer turns to for help with her homework.

Jennifer Wilson is the poor little rich girl. Her parents are divorced, and all the charge cards and clothes in the world can't make up for it. Jennifer's tall and thin, with cocoa-colored skin and a body that's made for all those designer clothes she wears.

April Winter has been to ten schools in the last ten years—and she hopes she's at Murphy to stay. Her energy, blond hair, and offbeat personality make her a standout at school.

And there's Dave Hunter, Brian Wu, and the rest of the gang. You'll meet them all in the halls of Murphy High and after school for a pizza at 18 Pine St.

The Diary

PINE

One

"Jennifer! Please turn around and face the front. I won't ask you again," said Mrs. Parisi sternly.

Sarah Gordon stole a look at Jennifer Wilson. She hated to see her friend get in trouble, but the history teacher had already warned her twice about talking in class. Jennifer turned toward the teacher with a meek look on her pretty face. Sarah wondered if the teacher was fooled.

It was one of those days when every student at Murphy High seemed to have trouble concentrating. It was Friday, and everyone's mind was on Saturday. Even Sarah, who rarely had trouble staying alert in Mrs. Parisi's history class, was affected. She found herself staring out the window at the bright snow-covered

1

playing fields. Pay attention, girl! she told herself.

"As I was saying," said Mrs. Parisi, opening a cardboard box on her desk, "we learn a lot about our past from what historians call primary sources. A primary source is an original document from a given time: a newspaper, a letter, a contract." She looked at Sarah. "What's another example of a primary source?"

"Birth records?" Sarah ventured.

"Good one," said Mrs. Parisi. "Anybody else?"

"Tax records," shouted someone.

"Old advertisements!"

"The captain's log!" shouted Russell Smith, a devoted *Star Trek* fan. The class laughed.

"You are all correct," said Mrs. Parisi, pleased. "And we've only scratched the surface. There are store inventory lists, bank records, opinion polls, notes of meetings, and so on. All are important historical documents. In fact, I have a friend who studied old restaurant menus to find out how our eating habits have changed—as well as the prices!"

Mrs. Parisi pulled a handful of different-colored journals out of the box on her desk. "Which brings us to our next project," she said, handing the notebooks to the first row of students. "Dave, can you help me pass out the rest of these?"

Sarah watched Dave Hunter unfold his long legs from under the desk and move to the front of the room. Dave was one of the best basketball players at Murphy High. His movements were smooth and graceful, whether he was running across the court to intercept a layup or guiding Sarah across a dance floor. Like Sarah's, his skin was a rich shade of brown, and she knew they made a handsome pair, even though she was almost a foot shorter than his six feet plus. He gave Sarah a crooked smile and a soft bump with his hip as he dropped a notebook onto her desk.

"For the next two weeks, we will use these notebooks for a special project," Mrs. Parisi went on. "I am going to ask each of you to keep a diary."

Sarah heard Jennifer groan softly.

"Who knows?" The teacher shrugged. "A hundred years from now, it may help a historian piece together what life was like for a sixteen-year-old in the twentieth century."

"A diary?" moaned Lowell Mizner, who sat in the front row. "Do the guys have to write one, too? I mean, do we have to write down our *feelings*?" He said the word sarcastically.

"Do you think only girls keep diaries, Lowell?" said Sarah. Other girls began to challenge him as well.

Lowell folded his arms and looked at them defiantly. "Look," he said, "my sister keeps a diary, and all she writes about is how many calories she ate that day, and how her boyfriend kisses her. Boring!"

Mrs. Parisi smiled. "It must have been interesting enough if you found the need to read it," she said.

Lowell turned bright pink. "Guys don't keep diaries," he insisted.

"Are you saying that Christopher Columbus and Thomas Jefferson were not guys?" Sarah chimed in.

3

"They kept journals."

"They were famous," another boy pointed out. "They had something important to write about."

"Maybe you're right," said Mrs. Parisi, her eyes sparkling. Sarah looked at her, surprised. "Everyone must keep a diary," the history teacher continued, "but the boys may call theirs a 'daily journal' if they prefer." She looked at Lowell with a smile. "In a daily journal, you don't have to write down how many calories you ate or whom you kissed!"

Everyone laughed, and Lowell's face turned pink again. He looked as if he wanted to respond, but Mrs. Parisi's warning glance told him the subject was closed. She went to the blackboard and began to write down the details of the diary assignment.

While Mrs. Parisi's back was turned, a square piece of paper landed on Sarah's desk. Sarah quickly put it under her books and looked around to see who might have sent it. Dave was busy taking notes, but Jennifer had a big smile on her face.

"Open it," Jennifer whispered.

Sarah unfolded the note slowly, flinching whenever the paper crackled. Her friend had drawn a caricature of Mrs. Parisi with her mouth open wide. The students were drawn with their heads thrown back and Zs coming out of their mouths. Jennifer had drawn herself sprawled out on her desk, with the largest Zs emanating from her. "Hey, girl, is this class boring or what?" she had written at the bottom. "If I wanted a naptime, I would have stayed in kindergarten!" There followed

4

almost two full pages of gossip, plans for the weekend, and a description of the gorgeous boy Jennifer had seen at the mall.

After reading it, Sarah carefully folded the note under her desk and gave her friend a tolerant smile. "One of these days, you're going to get caught," Sarah whispered. When she turned to the front again, she found Mrs. Parisi looking straight at her.

"Sarah, I asked you a question."

"I'm sorry," said Sarah. She felt her face getting hot as she left the note on her lap and reached for her pencil. Mrs. Parisi repeated the question. Luckily, it was about yesterday's homework, and Sarah had no trouble answering it.

But a few moments later, Mrs. Parisi had to stop her lecture again. In the back of the room, a group of boys were laughing. "What is it with you people today?" she asked her class.

"Sorry, Mrs. Parisi," said one of the boys, "but look." He pointed to the back corner of the room. Sarah looked along with the others and saw one of her classmates dozing with her head on her desk. Julie O'Connor, a quiet African-American girl who never spoke up in class, had fallen asleep over her textbook. The class giggled as they watched her back gently rise and fall with each breath.

"If she snores, I'm going to lose it!" Lowell whispered loudly.

"That's enough, Lowell," said Mrs. Parisi. She ordered the class to face the front of the room. "As I was saying!" she said very loudly.

But Julie's head stayed down. The teacher walked to the back of the room and tried nudging her gently, but the girl remained hunched over her desk. Mrs. Parisi looked upset. She quickly called the nurse over the intercom, and the class waited, murmuring nervously.

The nurse arrived, and some of the students stood up out of their seats to get a better view of Julie, but Mrs. Parisi ordered them to sit down again. Sarah watched as the nurse first tried shaking Julie awake. When that didn't work, she broke an ammonia capsule and waved it under Julie's nose. Julie made a face and exhaled loudly. She looked up to find the eyes of the entire class on her, and quickly put her head down again.

Sarah felt sorry for Julie and looked away. The nurse insisted that Julie leave the class and accompany her to the office. As soon as the two had left, the class began to chatter excitedly.

"You think she was high on something?" said Russell.

"Maybe she's on medication," said Lisa Norton. "I have a cousin who's got epilepsy, and if he doesn't take his pills, he passes out."

"Naw. In epilepsy, you go into wild fits," said Lowell.

"That's not true!" Lisa cried. "Some people do, but not everyone has that kind of epilepsy."

"It's not a good idea to try to figure out what happened," Mrs. Parisi interrupted. "That's how rumors get started. Let's get back to the assignment, shall we?" But when the bell rang a few moments later, the class was still talking about the episode.

"I'll bet everyone writes about this in their diary tonight," Sarah told Jennifer as they left the class.

"I guess that picture I drew was right after all," said Jennifer, smoothing her white blouse and blue wool slacks. The matching jacket had silver rose-shaped buttons. Sarah had never seen the outfit before, but that didn't surprise her. Jennifer had more clothes than almost anyone at Murphy High. "Julie sure looked sleepy this morning."

"Yo, Jennifer, about these notes you keep passing me," Sarah began.

But Jennifer wasn't listening. "More work!" she said, waving her notebook. "She must think I don't have other classes."

"I thought you liked diaries," said Sarah. "Don't you keep one?"

"Sure, but I don't write in it every single day," Jennifer said, dropping the notebook into her leather bookbag. "It's different when you're *forced* to do it!"

They were out in the hallway when they heard Mrs. Parisi's voice rising over the sounds of milling students. "Jennifer, may I see you for a minute?"

"Dang! What does she want?" Jennifer muttered. She squeezed Sarah's shoulder and walked back to the classroom. "I'll catch up with you at 18 Pine," she called back.

"Jennifer got busted, huh?" said Dave, falling in

step with Sarah. He switched his books to his right hand to put his arm around her.

"I'm surprised Mrs. Parisi didn't call *me* back, too," said Sarah.

"Parisi wouldn't chew you out. You're her best student," said Dave. "You always hand in your homework on time, and you always speak up in class."

"If I'm so good," said Sarah, stopping at her locker, "how come you got one point more on last week's quiz than I did?"

Dave rubbed his fingernails on his shirt and smiled modestly. "I guess she was grading good looks that day."

"Spare me, Dave!" Sarah said, laughing. But as they continued down the hall, Sarah couldn't help thinking that if Mrs. Parisi *had* graded on looks, Dave would have gotten an A-plus.

The 18 Pine St. pizzeria was a popular place to grab an after-school snack, and the place was crowded with students when Sarah and her cousin Tasha arrived. Mr. and Mrs. Harris waved to the Gordon cousins as the girls made their way to their favorite booth to drop off their coats. When they returned to the counter, Mr. Harris had Tasha's diet cola and Sarah's medium orange soda waiting.

"We're getting predictable, huh, Mr. Harris?" said Tasha, handing him a five-dollar bill.

"I know my regulars," he said, giving her the change. "Besides, there's nothing wrong with being predictable, is there?"

"There is for my cousin," Sarah told him.

Tasha had moved in with Sarah's family after her parents died in a car crash, and from the start she had been anything but predictable. Tasha had light brown skin, ebony hair, and eyes that reflected every one of her moods. Her basketball skills had gotten her on the Murphy High girls' team, and she had soon become one of the most popular girls in the school.

Sarah, on the other hand, didn't like being the center of attention. One-on-one conversations with close friends were more her style. While their friends liked Tasha for her energy and intelligence, they admired Sarah's even temperament and common sense.

"Are you going out with Dave tonight?" asked Tasha, swirling the ice in her cup.

"Of course," said Sarah. "A guy Dave met in basketball camp is throwing a party, and we are going to dance our butts off!" Before she could ask Tasha what her plans were for that night, Kwame Brown and José Melendez joined them.

Kwame took a seat in the booth next to Tasha and gave her a sly wink. "Is Billy coming?" he asked her. Billy Simpson was the captain of the football team, and Tasha dated him often.

"No, he stayed after school to work out in the weight room," Tasha replied.

"Good, because I want to sit next to you, and I'd hate to have to jack him up," Kwame said, clenching his fists. The idea of Kwame beating up muscular Billy

9

Simpson was ridiculous, and they all laughed.

Sarah turned toward José and found him smiling mysteriously at her. The two had gone out a few times before discovering that just being friends was better for both of them. Sarah noticed he had kept his jacket on. He peeked into the zippered opening.

"What are you looking at, José?" Sarah asked.

José grinned and was about to reply when Mr. Harris brought the plate of onion rings he had ordered. José sat very still until Mr. Harris left; then he picked up an onion ring and waved it over the opening of his jacket. Something inside moved toward the food. Sarah and Tasha watched until the pink nose of a kitten poked out.

"How adorable!" Tasha cried.

"Shhh!" Kwame and José chorused.

"You know how Mr. Harris gets about pets," said Kwame.

"He's got a good reason," Sarah pointed out. "Remember when he kicked out that guy with the dog? He told us if the Board of Health found an animal on the premises, they could give him a big fine."

The kitten showed no interest in the onion ring. Instead, he mewed softly and struggled to get out of the jacket. He was light gray, with darker gray stripes, and looked as if he had just woke up.

"This is Kirby," said José, bending down to kiss the nose of the cat.

"He's adorable," Tasha repeated.

"You want him?"

10

"I'd love to have him, but my uncle is allergic," said Tasha. Sarah nodded in agreement. She could just hear her father letting out one of his explosive sneezes at the sight of the kitten.

"That's the trouble with kittens," said José gloomily. "Everybody thinks they're wonderful, but no one will take one."

"How did *you* end up with him?" asked Sarah.

José sighed and told his friends about the stray cat he had found the month before. "I thought she looked a little chubby, but she had long hair, and I didn't think she was pregnant," he said. "Everybody loved Reina—that means queen in Spanish—but now that she's a mother, she went from being the family cat to being my cat. I'm supposed to find homes for Kirby and his five brothers and sisters."

When April Winter and Steve Adams walked in with Jennifer, the three were also introduced to Kirby.

April's blue eyes looked sad as she watched the kitten tumble around inside José's jacket. "I'd love to have him, but my stepmother says no pets except goldfish until after the baby is born."

"What about you, Steve?" said José. The kitten had reached the opening of the jacket again and was looking directly at Steve.

Steve ran his fingers through his red hair and looked at the kitten. "I don't know...."

"He's healthy, fun, and full of pep," said José, stroking the spot between Kirby's ears with two fingers.

"Let me talk to my parents," Steve said.

11

"Hey, my first 'maybe,'" said José with a grin. The grin quickly faded. "That leaves me with five more to go."

"Did you put an ad in the paper?" asked Jennifer.

José nodded. "No replies yet."

"If that doesn't work, there's always the SPCA," Jennifer pointed out.

"You can't leave them there!" April cried. "The SPCA will just destroy them."

"They'll try to find a home for them first," Jennifer retorted. "Besides, what happens if José can't find owners? Should he let them go free?"

"All I know is, this is her last litter," José vowed. "I'm going to get her neutered."

"You mean spayed," Tasha corrected. "Neutered is for males, spayed is for females."

"Whatever," said José. "If Reina wants more kittens, she's going to have to adopt!"

His friends laughed loudly, but they quieted down when Mr. Harris came out of the supply room nearby. "What's the joke?" he asked amiably.

"Just school stuff," Tasha replied casually. José zipped his jacket up all the way to his chin.

After Mr. Harris returned to his counter, Kwame pointed at José. "You should have seen the look on your face, man." He imitated José's panic-stricken expression. "You looked like the guy on the poster for that movie *Dragon Blood*."

"Billy and I are going to see that tonight up at the college," Tasha announced.

"I heard that movie was really gory," said Kwame.

Steve nodded. "It's the goriest movie ever made," he said solemnly. "I read somewhere that they used a hundred gallons of fake blood in just one scene!"

"Ugh," said Sarah, shuddering.

"I read about a guy in California who is suing the theater because he's had nightmares ever since he saw it," said April.

The table got quiet. Suddenly an icy hand gripped the back of Sarah's neck. Sarah shrieked and whirled around. She saw Dave with a surprised look on his face. "Don't you ever sneak up on me like that!" she scolded him.

"I was just saying hi," he said. "I guess my hand was cold from being outside." When he found out what they had been discussing, he grinned. "Hey, if you want to go to that movie instead of the party..."

Sarah shook her head. "No thanks."

"Well, you all have a good time tonight," said Jennifer with a loud sigh.

"What will you be doing?"

"Homework," said Jennifer irritably. "My mom is on this crusade to get my grades up. She thinks she's not paying enough attention to me, so now she wants to see my homework. And Friday is her only free night."

"That's rough," said Steve.

"What did Mrs. Parisi want when she called you back to class?" Sarah asked.

"Not much." Jennifer sighed. "She told me to pay

more attention in class. Hey, I wasn't the one who passed out!"

"Who passed out?" asked April.

Jennifer told her friends about Julie O'Connor.

"That's nothing," said Tasha. "When I lived in Oakland, one of the kids ate some kind of mushroom to get high, and he began to hallucinate in the middle of class. He said we all looked like skeletons to him."

"How come that stuff never happens in my classes?" complained José.

Tasha's expression was grim. "Believe me, José, seeing that guy freak out was terrible. You're *lucky* you weren't there."

"And you wouldn't want to be in Mrs. Parisi's class either," Jennifer assured him, tapping her wire-bound notebook. She turned to Dave. "When are we supposed to find the time to write a diary?"

"I don't know anything about that," Dave reminded her. "I'm working on a *daily journal*, remember?"

"It sounds like an interesting project," said Kwame. His favorite subject was American history. "I hope Mrs. Parisi gives us that assignment next year."

"A huge waste of time, if you ask me," said Jennifer crossly. "Nobody cares about our lives. Besides, how much history can you get out of a diary?"

"Lots," said Kwame, warming up to the subject. His friends in the booth groaned. It didn't take much to get him started on a history lesson.

"Quick! Somebody throw him an onion ring!" Tasha cried.

"If you all be quiet, you might learn something," Kwame said.

But before he could get started, Tasha nudged her cousin and pointed to the picture windows at the front of the pizza shop. Just visible in the fading daylight was the silhouette of a young girl. The girl was in a hurry, and she quickly disappeared past the windows. Still, the glimpse was enough. Sarah recognized her younger sister, Allison.

"Isn't she supposed to be grounded?" asked Tasha.

Sarah nodded. "Dad said she had to come straight home all week. Where is that girl going?"

"Only one way to find out," said Tasha, putting her coat on and heading for the front door.

Sarah found her coat and followed her cousin. "We'll be right back," she told the others.

Kwame watched them leave, then looked back at his remaining friends. Obviously they'd forgotten all about the subject of diaries. Instead they were playing with the kitten and keeping a wary eye on Mr. and Mrs. Harris. "Class dismissed," Kwame muttered.

Two

When Tasha and Sarah dashed outside, they spotted Allison walking briskly ahead of them. But the streets were crowded with people leaving work, and it was hard to keep her in sight. Allison turned the corner at Union Street, and Sarah speeded up, nearly colliding with a burly man.

"Easy, cuz," said Tasha, grabbing her cousin just in time. "Instead of trying to catch up, let's hang back and see where she goes."

"She's not going home like she's supposed to," said Sarah. "That's all that matters to me."

"You make her sound like she's in nursery school," said Tasha. "Allison is twelve years old."

They followed as Allison walked along Union Street, which gradually sloped down toward the river.

She turned another corner, and Sarah broke into a run again. But Tasha was the better athlete, and she reached the end of the block first. She peered around the corner, then turned to Sarah with a wide grin. "Looks like she's got company."

Allison had stopped in front of a McDonald's and was talking to a boy. Until that moment, Sarah had never heard her sister talk about boys or give any indication that she was interested in them. She was surprised to see Allison alone with one. She was even more astonished when the boy leaned forward to give Allison a kiss.

"Did you see that?" Sarah demanded.

Tasha grabbed her arm. "Hold it, Sarah. Let's just leave them alone. This is her last day of being grounded. Give her a break."

"What are you talking about?" said Sarah. "Why do you want to see her get away with this? She's not obeying my parents' rules."

Tasha smiled. "What about last week when you came back after midnight from your date with Dave? Friday night, your curfew is twelve o'clock sharp. Aren't you glad your parents didn't find out about that?"

"I was only a half hour late," Sarah protested. "Besides, I'm sixteen. Allison is just a kid."

They looked back, but Allison and the boy had disappeared into the McDonald's.

"I've seen enough," said Tasha. "How about you?"

"All right," said Sarah, still unsure. "Let's go."

As they walked up Union Street, Tasha laughed. "You know what's really good about this?" she said with a wicked grin. "Now we have something on Allison. She won't be able to blackmail us when *we* come back after curfew."

"That helps you more than me." Sarah nudged her cousin. "I'm late once in a while, but you're always coming back late from a date."

"Midnight is an unreasonable curfew for girls our age," said Tasha. "Jennifer gets to stay out until one in the morning."

"You know what Dad says about that: 'If you want to stay out another hour, leave an hour earlier,'" said Sarah, imitating her father's voice.

Tasha shook her head. "It's not the same thing at all, and he knows it."

When they returned to 18 Pine St., Jennifer had already gone home, and the others had their coats on.

"We're going to my place to print up some fliers about Kirby and the others," said Steve, gesturing at José, Kwame, and April.

"Let's get going. I gotta get Kirby out of my jacket pretty soon," said José. He winced suddenly. "He keeps digging his claws into my shirt to climb up."

"Are you sure he has enough air in there?" said April. "Maybe he's suffocating."

"No way, he's fine," said José. He lowered the zipper of his jacket an inch just to make sure.

It was all the room Kirby needed. The kitten jumped out and landed on the table. He ran toward the now-

19

empty basket of onion rings, then scurried toward the napkin dispenser as José reached for him.

"There he goes!" cried Steve.

"Get him!" José shouted.

Dave's reflexes were the quickest of all, and he had the kitten in his large hands in no time. He turned Kirby over to José, who returned him to his jacket.

"What's all the fuss about?" asked Mrs. Harris.

"No problem," said José just as Kirby dug his claws into his shirt. He winced and grabbed his stomach as Mrs. Harris gave him a suspicious look.

"You all right?" she said.

"Yes," said José between breaths. "Just...uh, some indigestion. I guess I ate those onion rings too fast."

"I'll get you some Alka-Seltzer," said Mrs. Harris.

"That's okay," said José quickly. "We were just heading out."

Kirby meowed.

José's smile froze on his face.

Mrs. Harris's eyebrows shot up knowingly. "Go on, then," she said slowly. Suddenly she put her hand on his jacket where Kirby was moving about. "It's a good thing my husband didn't catch you with that...indigestion."

"Yes, ma'am," said José, turning a deep shade of red. He zipped his jacket up high and headed for the door. The others followed him, stifling their laughter as they went.

* * *

20

When the Gordon cousins got home that evening, the family had started dinner without them.

"Oops," said Tasha under her breath. Her uncle liked to have everyone together at mealtimes, even if it didn't always work out that way. As principal of Hamilton High, a school for students with special needs, Mr. Gordon worked long hours, and so did Mrs. Gordon, who was a lawyer. Even the girls' grandmother, Miss Essie, was often busy with her career. She was an actress who did commercials and took roles at local theaters.

"Just in time for dessert," Mr. Gordon grumbled.

"Sorry, Dad," said Sarah quickly. "We thought Dave had his car and could give us a ride. We ended up taking the bus."

"A likely story!" said Allison.

"Allison," warned Mrs. Gordon.

Allison looked down and resumed eating, but she had a gleeful smile on her face.

Tasha and Sarah headed to the kitchen to wash their hands. "Did you see her gloating?" Tasha muttered. "I've got half a mind to tell on her!"

"Me too," Sarah whispered back.

Between large helpings of Miss Essie's famous collard greens, Sarah told her family about Julie O'Connor and the diary project.

Allison giggled. "A diary! High school sounds so *hard*," she said sarcastically.

"Your daughter has a mouth on her," Miss Essie told

Mr. and Mrs. Gordon. She tried to sound stern, but Sarah knew her grandmother better. Allison was her baby, and everything Allison did was either wonderful or quickly forgiven.

"I don't know where she gets her behavior from," said Mr. Gordon, looking at his mother innocently.

"Don't make me tell, Donald," Miss Essie replied.

"What kind of stuff are you going to put in your diary?" Allison asked.

"Everything that happens to me," said Sarah.

"Bor-ing!" Allison murmured into her plate.

Sarah nudged Tasha's leg under the table and turned back to her younger sister. "For example, today I went to that McDonald's off Union Street to meet my boyfriend. Now that's pretty interesting—wouldn't you say?"

Allison almost dropped her fork. When she looked at Sarah, there was a hint of panic in her eyes, but she didn't say anything. And for the rest of the evening, she was unusually quiet.

After the dinner plates were cleaned up, Sarah ran upstairs to get ready for her date with Dave. She was on the telephone with her best friend, Cindy Phillips, when she heard a car pull into the driveway. She took one last look at herself in the hall mirror and checked the back of her printed silk shirt to see if it was tucked in straight inside her jeans.

When she opened the door, it was not Dave but Billy Simpson, coming to pick up Tasha. He hugged

Sarah with his beefy arms and walked in.

"Is she ready?" Billy asked, looking up the stairs

"She'll be right down," said Sarah, closing the door.

Billy noticed the silk blouse and gave her an appreciative nod. "Looks like you are stepping out tonight."

"You'd better look at *me* like that!" said·Tasha from the top of the stairs. She came downstairs wearing tight black jeans, a red shirt, and a black vest. Then she grabbed her uncle's leather bomber jacket from the closet. It was much too big for her, but it seemed to work. *Anything* seemed to work if Tasha was wearing it, Sarah thought.

It was past nine when Dave finally rang the doorbell. "Sorry I'm late," he told Sarah.

"Did you get lost on the way over?" Sarah asked coolly. Dave smiled. He and Sarah had lived across the street from each other since they were kids.

"Mom had the car," he said, shrugging. "It was out of my hands."

"You could have called," said Sarah.

"Hey, I said I was sorry."

Sarah nodded but didn't say anything. Things were starting off poorly, and she didn't want to make them worse. She expected the party to be in full swing when they arrived, but instead the apartment was half empty. Music was blaring from the speakers, but it wasn't anything to dance to. Dave soon found his friend Lee, and the two began to gossip about basketball players they knew from camp.

"I'm going to find something to drink," Sarah told

23

Dave after listening to them as long as she could stand. "You want something?"

"Sure, a Coke," said Dave quickly. He went back to his conversation, and Sarah went to look for drinks. She found a bowl of cheese curls on the living room coffee table, but getting a handful meant reaching around a couple who sat on the sofa kissing passionately. Next to the sofa, a tall, slim man leaned against the wall behind a table of sodas and liquor. Like almost everyone else at the party, he seemed a lot older than Sarah and Dave.

"Hello, beautiful," he said, winking at her. "What's your pleasure?"

"Two Cokes," said Sarah.

"That all? Sure I can't add something to liven them up for you?" He held up a bottle of rum.

"Just Coke," Sarah said firmly.

"Two dollars," said the man as he handed her two Styrofoam cups. He saw the look of surprise on Sarah's face. "Didn't Lee tell you?" he said. "It's a cash bar."

"Lee didn't tell me," said Sarah. "My purse is in the other room."

"Tell you what: for a beautiful lady like you, they're on the house."

There was something creepy about this guy. "That's okay," Sarah replied. "I'll get my purse."

She found Dave, who was still talking to his friend. When she pulled him away from Lee, he looked annoyed.

24

"What's up?" said Dave. "Where's my Coke?"

"Look, I don't know if I want to stay here," said Sarah. "The music isn't very good. And believe it or not we have to pay for the sodas."

"We just got here. Give me a few more minutes, then we'll go, okay?" said Dave as he pulled out his wallet and handed her two bills.

There is no place to hide at a dull party, Sarah realized. After she paid the man and grabbed the sodas, she gave one to Dave and then wandered from room to room. At one point, she joined a cluster of girls who had started dancing, but they all seemed to know each other and Sarah felt out of place. Ten minutes later, she returned to the spot where she had left Dave. He was no longer talking to Lee, but to the slim man who had served her the sodas.

"Sarah, I want you to meet Donell Maines," Dave said. "He's the assistant coach at Madison Community College."

"My pleasure," said Donell with a wink. Sarah couldn't ignore his outstretched hand, and she shook it. She squirmed when he turned her hand over and kissed the top of it. Dave looked on and smiled.

"He gave me the creeps," Sarah told Dave later as they drove home. After the unwelcome kiss, it had taken Dave another twenty minutes to decide he had had enough of the party. By then, Sarah was seriously thinking about calling a cab.

"Donell ain't so bad," said Dave.

25

"That's your opinion," Sarah retorted.

They drove through downtown Madison in silence. Sarah stared out at the display windows in the big department stores that flew by.

A few blocks from home, Dave finally spoke. "You still mad about the party?" he asked.

Sarah sighed. "I'm not mad, just frustrated. You were the only one I knew there, and you ignored me all night. How did you expect me to have a good time?"

"I haven't seen some of these guys since last summer," said Dave. "You could have danced."

"To that junk?"

"You can't blame me for the bad tunes," Dave snapped.

In front of the Gordons' house, Dave stopped the car and turned off the ignition. In the darkness they stared at each other for a long time.

Finally Dave mumbled, "I'm sorry. I acted like a jerk tonight."

Sarah leaned toward him and gave him a hug. "No you didn't," she replied. "You were more like an imbecile."

Dave laughed, and Sarah could smell his cologne mixed with his sweet breath. The tension evaporated, and they moved closer, then kissed for a long time.

Sarah pulled away. She looked into his dark brown eyes and at the handsome face illuminated by the streetlight.

"You want to drive around a little?" he asked.

Sarah considered it for a moment. "I'd better go . . . ."

26

"Sure." Dave sounded sad. "Hey," he said abruptly, "you're not going to write about what happened tonight, are you? In that diary we're supposed to keep?"

"Why not?" said Sarah.

"Come on," he said impatiently. "It was a lousy date, and it's going to make me look bad."

"It wasn't totally lousy," said Sarah. She grinned. "I like the way it ended. Don't worry about the diary," she said. "I'll treat you with respect."

Dave got out of the car and walked her to the front door. He gave her a final kiss. "Next time we go to a party, it will be different. I guarantee it."

"Better be," warned Sarah.

By midnight, Sarah had changed into her nightshirt and climbed into bed. No trouble making curfew tonight, she thought.

She took the spiral notebook from the nightstand and opened it to the first page. What was she going to write about? Did Mrs. Parisi really want them to write about their own lives for history class? It seemed so unimportant, but maybe it would be as the teacher had said, some kind of record of what a teenager's life was like.

"Friday. 12:05 A.M. Where do I begin?" she wrote. The day's events replayed themselves when she closed her eyes. She picked up her pen again and continued her entry.

I love going out with Dave—he is the coolest guy I

know. And usually he's so nice. But tonight he acted like a jerk. He showed up late, then proceeded to ignore me most of the night, just so he could hang out talking to those guys he knows from basketball. Sometimes I just don't get men! At least we made up when he dropped me off.

Sarah went on writing in the journal, describing what had happened in history class with Julie and how she and Tasha had followed Allison to the McDonald's. *I can't believe my baby sister has a boyfriend!*

It was past one A.M. when Sarah finally put down her pen. She heard the front door closing softly and a car driving away from the house. Moments later Tasha knocked softly on her door.

"What are you doing still up?" whispered Tasha.

"Just writing," said Sarah. She glanced at the clock. "It must have been a long movie," she added teasingly. Tasha grinned and nodded.

"They weren't up late waiting for me, were they?" Tasha said, gesturing toward Mr. and Mrs. Gordon's bedroom down the hall.

"You're free and clear," said Sarah. "Just remember: When you go to the bathroom, don't—"

"I know, I know," Tasha interrupted, "you were going to say, 'Don't run the water too long because of the noise.' I won't. 'Night." She closed Sarah's door softly.

Three

Kwame held up a forkful of cafeteria food. "Can you believe this was once a chicken?"

"Thanks for the reminder, Kwame," Sarah replied. She pushed aside the chicken and rice on her tray and dug into the applesauce instead. Her left hand rested on her notebook. She had not let the diary out of her sight since Friday night.

"Did you get started on that?" Jennifer asked, pointing to the notebook.

"Yeah," said Sarah. "It's not that bad once you get going. It's actually kind of fun."

"Please, girl!" said Jennifer with a short laugh.

29

"It's true," said Sarah. "How about you?"

"I'll get it done somehow," said Jennifer vaguely.

When José arrived, he handed Sarah and Jennifer a sheet of yellow paper. "Check out this flier," he said. "Steve and I put them up all over town."

The flyer showed a computer-drawn cat. "Single gray feline seeks owner. I am the kitten of your dreams. I like company, attention, and a little catnip now and then. Hurry! I'm very lonely!"

"How cute!" Sarah exclaimed. "Did anybody call?"

"Two calls, but they were just kids," José admitted. "But all we need is five calls and we're in business—I mean, out of business," he said brightly. "Steve's parents took Kirby."

Steve grinned. "It was love at first sight."

"Like you and me?" April said teasingly.

Steve flushed bright red.

Kwame looked up as Billy and Tasha came over to the table. "How was *Dragon Blood*?" he asked.

"Great!"

"Boring!"

"It was boring," Tasha insisted as Billy glared at her. "It has a lot of blood and gore, but no suspense."

"She doesn't know what she's saying," said Billy, waving Tasha away. "It's about this dude who finds an old bottle. He thinks it's wine, but it's really dragon's blood!" He proceeded to tell Kwame and Steve the entire plot of the film, his arms flailing wildly at times. "At the end, he has to rescue his girlfriend by killing this giant, slimy thing!"

"Don't listen to him," Tasha said. "The monster looked like a garden slug. I don't know why that guy in California who tried to sue the theater got nightmares," she said, shaking her head. "The movie is so silly."

"Maybe he had a garden," said Cindy.

Tasha and Sarah laughed.

At the other end of the table, Jennifer and Kwame were talking in hushed tones. Sarah watched as Kwame pushed his glasses up on his nose. "I don't know," he said slowly. "I don't want to do your homework for you."

"It's not homework," Jennifer insisted. "It's a special project. We're supposed to keep it anonymous, so she can't even grade it."

Sarah was about to speak up. She didn't think Mrs. Parisi had said that, but she wasn't sure. She had missed a lot of the instructions because she had been distracted by Jennifer's note.

Kwame still looked doubtful. "I think you'd better do it yourself," he said finally.

"Maybe you're right, Kwame," said Jennifer. She took back the wire-bound notebook. "I'm sorry I asked."

"That's okay," said Kwame. "could turn out to be an interesting assignment, you know."

"I'll just have to muddle through on my own," Jennifer said. "But could you help me a little? You help other people with their homework." Kwame nodded at that, and Jennifer pressed on. "You see, I know what I want to say, but I don't know how to put it in words." She gazed at him with her pretty eyes.

"As long as you're the one who's recounting it," said Kwame. "I don't think it would be a problem to help you figure out how to put it down."

"Do you think you could come over to my house this afternoon?" Jennifer asked sweetly.

"Sure," Kwame agreed.

Sarah couldn't believe what she was hearing. As the cafeteria bell rang, she ran up to Jennifer and grabbed her arm. "What are you going to do with Kwame?"

"Nothing," said Jennifer. "He offered to help me write the diary. I don't think there's anything wrong with that." She shook off Sarah's arm and headed off into the hallway, which was overflowing with students.

Cindy caught up to Sarah, and the two watched Jennifer go off.

"You know," Sarah told Cindy as they headed to class, "sometimes I wonder if there's a school where girls learn to play boys the way Jennifer plays Kwame."

"If there is, Jennifer is a teacher!" said Cindy.

"You've got that right," Sarah agreed.

That afternoon Sarah brought her diary to history class, expecting to turn it in. But as the period wore on, it became clear that Mrs. Parisi was not planning to discuss the diaries.

Sarah stole a glance at Julie O'Connor. She was relieved to see the girl back in school after what had happened on Friday. Julie looked better today, but she seemed fidgety. She tapped her pencil on her thigh and shifted around in her seat so often, it was difficult to ignore. When Mrs. Parisi glared at her, Julie stopped squirming, but moments later she was at it again.

"Don't forget to bring your diaries tomorrow," Mrs. Parisi said as the bell rang.

"Did you notice how strange Julie acted today?" Sarah asked Jennifer as they left class.

"Yeah," said Jennifer. "She looked like she had to go really bad."

Lisa Norton overheard them. "I talked to her about last Friday," she said.

"Does she have epilepsy, or something else?" asked Sarah.

"She told me she didn't get enough sleep the night before." Lisa frowned.

"I don't believe it for a minute. That girl was out *cold*."

Sarah didn't say anything, but silently she agreed with Lisa. Whatever was up with Julie had to be more than missed sleep.

At home that night, Allison was in trouble. Again.

"You didn't wait long to test your freedom," said Mr. Gordon, looking at his younger daughter. Sarah watched from the kitchen as Allison stood next to the front door, facing her father and grandmother with her jaw clenched.

"I want you home before dark, young lady, or you

33

call. Is that clear?" said Miss Essie.

"I was at Pam's house," said Allison. Pam was her best friend.

Mr. Gordon and Miss Essie traded surprised looks. "Allison, Pam was over here looking for you this afternoon," said Mr. Gordon.

"She was?" said Allison in astonishment.

Sarah observed the scene from the kitchen door. She could almost see her sister's mind struggling to get out of her lie. "I waited all afternoon at her house, and she was here waiting for me! Isn't that funny?" said Allison.

Sarah looked at her father. Did he believe Allison? she wondered. Mr. Gordon's face didn't reveal anything. He simply told Allison to wash up and get ready to eat.

At dinner, Mr. Gordon announced that he and Mrs. Gordon would have the TV in the den that evening to watch an address by the President.

After putting away the dishes, Sarah went straight to her bedroom. She prided herself on keeping it spotless—it was yet another way in which she and Tasha were complete opposites. So when she walked in, she knew immediately that something was wrong. Her closet door was slightly open, and there were definite wrinkles on her bedspread. Tasha must have been in here borrowing something, she thought. As she went to shut the closet door, something moved inside and Sarah nearly screamed.

There was Allison, cowering in a corner, under the

coat hangers.

"Allison, what are you doing in there?" Sarah demanded.

"I was looking for one of my T-shirts," said Allison. "Sometimes Miss Essie puts my stuff in your drawers."

"My drawers are on the other side of the bed," said Sarah. "Besides, if that was what you were doing, there wouldn't be any reason to be hiding in the closet."

Allison bit her lip, as if she were trying to think of another reason.

"You've been looking for my diary, haven't you?" asked Sarah.

"What diary?" said Allison.

"The one I've been talking about all week," Sarah replied hotly. "I'm not in the mood for this, Allison. If I catch you in here again, you'll be in serious trouble."

"How did you know I was at the McDonald's last Friday?" Allison demanded. Her expression shifted from guilty to desperate.

"So *that's* why—" Sarah began.

"Pam told you all about him, didn't she?" cried Allison. "She's a rat!"

"She is not," said Sarah. She quickly explained what Tasha and she had seen on Friday. "But don't worry: Tasha and I aren't going to tell anyone."

Allison looked at her older sister skeptically. "No one except your whole history class," she said, slamming the door as she left.

35

"What was that all about?" said Tasha, opening the door and walking into the room. She helped her cousin straighten the bedspread as Sarah explained.

Tasha frowned. "Did she find it?"

"No," said Sarah triumphantly. "I know my little sister. It's in a safe place."

"You haven't written anything about me, have you?" said Tasha, only half jokingly.

Sarah stiffened slightly. "Of course," she said truthfully. "You're my cousin. You're in there. But it's nothing terrible." Nothing too terrible, she added to herself. It was only stuff about Tasha's coming in late after her date last weekend and taking too long in the bathroom the other morning, things like that.

"I don't want your whole history class knowing my business," Tasha went on.

"But they wouldn't," said Sarah. Suddenly everyone seemed worried about what she was writing. First Dave, then Allison, and now Tasha, too. "Nobody will see this book except me and Mrs. Parisi. And you know she won't tell anyone." A thought occurred to Sarah. "Is that why you wouldn't tell me much about your date with Billy last Friday?"

Tasha bit her lip. " I was afraid it would end up being read over the P.A. system during homeroom!"

Sarah laughed. "I promise, cuz. Whatever it is, it will be between you and me."

"All right," said Tasha, lowering her voice. "Because I've been dying to tell you. *Dragon Blood* wasn't the only thing we saw that night."

36

"What do you mean?" Sarah asked.

Tasha made sure her cousin's door was closed before she began. "After the movie, we walked around the college campus, and we ran into these two drunk white college students picking on a black student. Billy ran up to them and told them to lay off. Then the two guys started coming after him."

"Mistake!" said Sarah. She had seen what Billy could do to opposing football players.

"Big mistake," Tasha agreed. "He knocked one down to the ground, and was wrestling with the other one when the campus police came up. The black guy—we never found out his name—told the police what was going on, and luckily they believed him."

"What happened to the white guys?" said Sarah.

"I don't know," said Tasha with a shrug. "The cops put them in the car, but they were probably let off somewhere near their dormitories."

"Why wouldn't you want to tell me?" said Sarah. "That makes a great story."

Tasha sighed. "When we got back to the car, Billy was really upset. He kept slamming his hand on the dashboard and saying, 'I should have knocked them out!' over and over. He was so mad at those white guys, he had tears in his eyes. Can you imagine Billy Simpson with tears in his eyes?" Sarah shook her head, and Tasha continued. "That's why I got home so late. He was really wired, and we drove around and talked for a long time. He made me swear not to tell the rest of the gang, so you have to keep it to yourself."

"I promise," said Sarah. "Billy was very brave to fight those bullies. I'm proud of him."

"I don't care if you put it in the diary, just don't tell anyone, okay?" said Tasha.

"I promise."

"Not even Cindy."

Sarah was surprised to hear her cousin say that. She knew Tasha felt a little competitive with Cindy because she was Sarah's best friend. But Tasha knew Cindy was trustworthy.

After Tasha left, Sarah crept up to the attic. She made her way to an old cast-iron pot, lifted the lid, and took out the notebook. Every day she brought the diary to school with her, but this was her hiding spot for when she had it at home. In the dim light of the bare bulb overhead, Sarah riffled through the pages. She was surprised at how much she had already written, and relieved that Allison had not found it. Actually, now that she reread the entries, she was glad *nobody* knew what was in the book. Sarah hadn't meant to write anything negative about anyone, but the truth was, the more she wrote, the less inhibited she had felt.

Friday

"Every time we're at 18 Pine, and I talk about something that happened to me, Tasha has to come up with an even better story of something that happened to her back in Oakland. I know it's because she's still insecure about being here in Madison, but WHY IS SHE STILL INSECURE?

38

Saturday
Mom had to go to the office this morning. She looked so tired when she was leaving. I wonder if she ever wishes she stayed home and didn't work. When I get a job, I'm going to make sure I spend a lot more time with my kids.

Sunday
Went to Dave's place to do some homework today, and Mrs. Hunter sold me a raffle ticket for her church. First prize is a quilt! I didn't really want to buy it, but what could I do?

We didn't get much homework done, but we did manage to kiss a lot in the kitchen. It was strange to be making out and hear Mrs. Hunter rehearsing for gospel choir in the next room.

Sarah replaced the iron lid on the pot and turned off the attic light. She made her way downstairs with the diary tucked under her arm. She sat down at her desk and opened the notebook to a clean page and wrote about Billy's fight with the college boys. When she was done, she decided to stick the diary under the mattress rather than hide it upstairs in the attic. There was no way Allison would find it there tonight—at least not while Sarah was sleeping on it.

Four

On Tuesday Mrs. Parisi waited until the last ten minutes of class before discussing the diaries. "Before we start, is there anyone in the class who did *not* bring his or her journal today?"

Sarah looked at Jennifer out of the corner of her eye.

Jennifer caught Sarah looking at her and smiled smugly. Obviously she'd gotten the assignment done—thanks to Kwame.

"Good," said Mrs. Parisi, pleased that nobody had spoken up. "The first project we will do is very simple. We're going to pretend we're historians from the year 2100. We'll discover the diaries, and we are going to examine them for clues about the twentieth century.

We'll start with the technology of our time."

The teacher moved up and down the rows of desks, handing out a worksheet that listed the names of dozens of common machines.

"See how many times these technologies are mentioned in the diaries."

Piece of cake, Sarah thought. She knew she had mentioned the phone and Dave's car at least twice in her entries.

"Now go ahead and switch diaries," said Mrs. Parisi.

Sarah wasn't sure she had heard correctly. She was about to ask the teacher to repeat what she had said, but then the other students sprang into action. She watched with mounting horror as the students exchanged diaries with their friends.

"Here you go," said Dave, dropping his notebook on her desk. He held his hand out for Sarah's.

Sarah's heart was beating wildly. "Did Mrs. Parisi say we were going to trade diaries?"

"Of course," said Dave. "Last Friday. She even wrote it on the board." He smiled. "You must have spaced out."

"I guess so," said Sarah. She held her diary even tighter. She couldn't give hers to Dave—she'd written that comment about his mother, not to mention all the details of their fight.

"Are you going to trade with Dave or me?" said Jennifer, holding out her diary.

Sarah glared at Jennifer. This is her fault, she

thought. I was too busy on Friday with that stupid note she passed me to pay attention to what was going on in class.

Dave looked puzzled as he stared at Sarah. "You okay?"

"Yes," said Sarah. "Dave, why don't you trade with Jennifer. I've already promised mine to someone else." She looked frantically around the room for someone—anyone—else.

"Who?" said Dave.

She spied Julie O'Connor, who was still just sitting at her desk. She wore a clean but faded cable-knit sweater over her thin frame and a pair of old jeans.

"Julie O'Connor," Sarah replied hastily.

"You know her?" asked Dave, looking at the girl in the corner.

"We were in the same art class last semester," said Sarah. She didn't tell him that Julie had been just as quiet and invisible in art class as she was here. Before Dave could reply, Sarah crossed the room, ignoring the surprised look on Julie's face. "Do you want to trade?"

"Okay," said Julie, barely above a whisper. She handed Sarah her diary.

When Sarah got back to her seat, she noticed that Dave was looking away from her.

"Your homework tonight is to fill out that worksheet and answer the three questions I've written at the bottom. Be sure to bring the borrowed diaries tomorrow so you can trade back and continue to write in your own," said Mrs. Parisi.

43

Sarah glanced back at Julie. The shy girl had opened Sarah's diary and seemed absorbed in it. Sarah began to open Julie's diary, then decided to shut it. You are not going to miss any more important announcements because you weren't paying attention, she told herself angrily.

The smell of the pizza at 18 Pine St. that afternoon was overpowering. Sarah looked up at the daily special board: garlic pizza. That explains it, she thought as she waved to Mr. Harris. She saw Robert Thornton at the back booth, joking around with Cindy and Tasha. Sarah quickly put Julie's diary in her bookbag. I'd better not tell Tasha about the switch, she said to herself.

"Guess who I saw getting into a car with Amanda Dennis and Linda Plunkett!" said Cindy as Sarah sat down. She didn't wait for Sarah to ask. "Marcia Dean!"

"I'm not surprised," said Sarah. "A girl like her would be happier with them anyway." Linda Plunkett and Amanda Dennis were members of the Murphy High pep squad, and they were always trying to stir up trouble among the 18 Pine St. friends.

"Here comes Marcia's 'ex,'" said Robert, pointing to the doorway, where Kwame was walking in with Jennifer. Kwame and Marcia had dated briefly before Kwame discovered that Marcia was a thief.

"Smell that wonderful garlic!" Kwame said dreamily as he sat down.

"It's too strong." Jennifer wrinkled her nose. "I just

know it's going to get into my clothes." She patted the angora sweater she wore.

"You can't have too much garlic," Kwame declared.

Cindy patted Kwame's back. "He's right." Cindy's Jamaican parents had given her a taste for spicy food—the spicier the better.

Dave did not show up at 18 Pine St. that afternoon, and Sarah wondered if he was upset about history class. He had been so eager to read her diary. Then she noticed that Jennifer and Kwame had Dave's diary opened to the first page. Sarah tried hard not to look at it, but even upside down, she could make out a few phrases: "mad at myself" and "Lee's party."

Jennifer suddenly gave a little yelp. "I promised to meet my mom after work today," she said as she put her coat back on.

"I'll drive you," said Robert, standing up as well. The two of them had been dating on and off for the last few months.

"Don't bother. It's just a block away," said Jennifer.

"Don't forget this," said Kwame, putting the worksheet into Dave's diary and handing it to her.

Jennifer looked at the unfinished homework and made a face. "We'll work on it at your place later," she said.

As soon as she was gone, Robert snatched the book from Kwame's grasp. "What has the girl written about me?" he said, grinning.

"Give it back!" cried Kwame.

"Don't read that, Robert; it's none of your busi-

45

ness," said Tasha.

"If there's something about me in it, it *is* my business," said Robert. He kept Kwame and Sarah at arm's length while he opened the book to the first page. "Hey, this isn't Jennifer's handwriting," he declared, tossing the diary back to Kwame.

"I was trying to tell you that," said Kwame irritably. "They traded diaries in class today."

"They did *what*?" said Tasha.

Sarah winced and stole a look at her cousin. Tasha's mouth was open in disbelief. Here it comes, she thought.

"Sarah, you promised!" Tasha cried. "You said it was just between you and the teacher."

"That's what I thought, but I was wrong," said Sarah miserably. "I'm sorry."

"Who's got yours?" Tasha demanded.

Sarah told her. "I gave it to her because she doesn't know any of us."

"I don't want a strange girl knowing my business," said Tasha hotly.

"The diary is not about you, it's about me," said Sarah.

"Did you write about what happened with Billy and me last Friday?" said Tasha.

"Sure, but—"

"That's all I need to know," said Tasha, picking up her coat and bookbag. "I trusted you," she said. She stormed toward the entrance of the pizza shop. Sarah followed her.

46

"Look, Tasha, I thought—"

Sarah stopped when she realized Tasha wasn't about to listen to her. Maybe her cousin would hear Sarah's side later, at home.

When Sarah returned to the table at 18 Pine, Kwame looked at her apologetically. "I know I said something that set her off, but I don't know what it was."

"It's not your fault," said Sarah. She sighed loudly and picked up her cup of orange soda. It was empty. She looked at it in surprise.

Robert gave her a sheepish grin. "I thought you two were leaving for good."

"Well, you were wrong, weren't you?" said Sarah coolly. She handed him the empty cup and gestured toward the counter.

As Robert went to refill the cup, Cindy gently squeezed her friend's arm. "You going to be okay, Sarah?"

"Yeah. Tasha will get over it," Sarah replied. She looked at Kwame, who was busy filling in Jennifer's worksheet. "I thought you and Jennifer were going to do it together," she said.

"It's just something to do," said Kwame absently. "Besides, this diary she's got is pretty interesting." He glanced at Sarah.

"Check out the look on Kwame's face," said Cindy. "Whose diary is it?"

"Never mind," said Kwame, closing the notebook.

"So, Kwame," Sarah began. "Is there something in there about me?"

"Not necessarily." Kwame stifled a grin. "He could be talking about another Sarah!"

"What does it say?" By now, Cindy was burning with curiosity.

"Ah-ah-ah," said Robert, setting the orange soda in front of Sarah. "You all gave me grief when I wanted to read it. 'Those are private thoughts, Robert,'" he said, mimicking Sarah's voice.

"This is different," said Sarah, reaching for the book. "Dave was going to trade diaries with me, anyway." She was surprised to see Kwame pulling it away from her.

"Robert is right," Kwame said. "Technically, it would be wrong for you to look at it."

"Technically," said Sarah impatiently, "you're not supposed to be looking at it either, Kwame. This is Jennifer's assignment, not yours."

Kwame thought about that a moment, then put the diary in his backpack. "Maybe so," he said firmly, "but two wrongs don't make a right."

Five

Friday
It was a nightmare come true!

That was the first sentence in Julie's diary, and from then on, Sarah was hooked. Obviously Julie had also missed Mrs. Parisi's announcement about trading journals—her entries seemed so private.

When I woke up in class, Lowell and Justin were staring at me, and I wanted to jump out the window. I told the nurse I hadn't gotten any sleep the night before, but she still called Mom. From now on, I'll force myself to eat something at lunch. It was so embarrassing.

Saturday

I saw Lettie's teacher at the mall. She said Lettie's behaving better with the other Down's syndrome kids, but she's still pretty rambunctious. Lettie cried like crazy on her first day at the new school, but she's happy now. I'm happy for her, but I hate running home after school to be there when she gets home.

Sunday

Dad found the math quiz in my room, and gave me grief about it. I said he shouldn't have been in my room, and he and Mom started yelling. "There are no secrets in this household," he said. Yeah, right! It's not about secrets, it's about privacy. I didn't eat much at dinner, and they looked worried. Good. Let them.

Monday A.M.
R. smiled at me. He got a haircut, I think.

Monday Afternoon

I took way too much C.! I was bouncing off the walls in school today, but at least I didn't pass out. I was still feeling the effects during voice class. Mr. Hannes said I should work on controlling my lower register, and to put more breath behind the notes. I tried, but he said I had to try harder. I've only got two lungs!!! The lesson went overtime, and Mom was mad because it means we had to pay Lettie's baby-sitter overtime. She doesn't say it, but I know she wants me to quit so I can be home after school with Lettie every day.

Tuesday
Mom said she was late for work twice last week because she has to make Lettie's breakfast. Now she's turning the chore over to me. They just keep piling it on.

Sarah looked up from Julie's diary and glanced at the clock. It was almost midnight.

The worksheet lay finished on her desk. Sarah had picked out a few references to technology—airplanes, buses, telephones, cars, radios, refrigerators, and washing machines—but it was Julie's descriptions of her life that intrigued Sarah. Reading about her younger sister Lettie, who had Down's syndrome, the voice lessons, and the troubles Julie was having with her parents was fascinating. It was also disturbing, Sarah realized. Julie seemed to use food as a weapon in her fights with her parents, and what was the mysterious "C" she had taken on Monday. Cocaine? Crack? That would certainly explain Julie's sleeping in class.

In her diary, Julie had also mentioned an older brother named Brian who was going to college in Kentucky. Mr. O'Connor had taken an extra job as a night watchman to help pay his tuition. Julie wrote that her parents were working hard to provide for Lettie's and Brian's needs, and she was getting lost in the shuffle.

Sarah closed the other girl's diary and got up from her desk to stretch. In many ways, Julie's life was like

51

her own, but there were huge differences, too. Sarah couldn't imagine her dad searching her room for bad test scores—Allison, maybe, but not her dad.

That girl can write, thought Sarah as she pulled the bedspread down. "Why is she so shy in school?" She closed her eyes and tried to picture Julie. She was very attractive, but she didn't seem to care how she looked. Her hair was always tied loosely in the back, and it had not been cut or styled in some time. To top it off, Julie walked hunched over, hiding the front of her body with her shoulders and the books she clutched in front of her. "There are so many ways she could fix herself up," Sarah said out loud. She knew that Julie's taking better care of herself would not improve her home life, but it might make Julie feel better about herself.

Sarah also wondered who "R" was. It was clearly someone Julie liked at Murphy High. Russell Smith? Robert Thornton? Recoe Walker?

The sound of water running through the pipes in the bathroom distracted her. At this hour, it was probably Tasha. They hadn't spoken to each other since this afternoon, when Tasha had discovered that Julie had her diary.

As Sarah climbed into bed, a sad thought occurred to her. She scanned Julie's diary from front to back to see if her hunch was correct, and was dismayed to find out it was.

Julie had written almost thirty pages in her diary, but not one of those pages mentioned any close friends. Not a single one, Sarah thought sadly. I have

tons of them. But were Tasha and Dave still among
them? she wondered.

18 PINE

Six

"Did you find homes for them yet?" April asked José as she placed her lunch tray next to his. It was Thursday afternoon, and the cafeteria was crowded, as usual.

Sarah had her own diary back again. Julie had returned it to her on Wednesday, when the class had turned in their worksheets. As they were exchanging notebooks, Sarah couldn't help noticing how tired Julie looked. Her eyes were bloodshot, too. Was that related to the "C" she had taken? Sarah wanted to invite Julie to sit with her friends, but she couldn't find her anywhere in the cafeteria.

"We found homes for two more kittens," José told April. "Three down, three to go." He took a long drink of chocolate milk and looked around the cafeteria for possible kitten owners.

"Maybe we need more fliers," said Steve.

"Where would we put them?" José asked. "We've already papered all of Murphy High's bulletin boards and most of Madison's telephone poles with the first batch." He ran his fingers through his black hair. "If these three aren't gone by Friday, it looks like they're headed for the animal shelter."

"You can't give up that easily!" April cried.

"Easily!" Steve and José echoed.

"Do you know how far we walked to put up those notices? My feet were frozen by the time I got home," said Steve. "Ask Kwame, he went with us."

They turned toward the sophomore, who was scribbling furiously in a notebook.

"Don't tell me you're still doing Jennifer's homework," said April.

"I promised I would help," said Kwame. "Besides, it's not like I'm doing everything. Jennifer told me what she wants written, and I'm writing it for her."

"Jennifer should do it all herself," Tasha declared as she joined them. "Isn't that right, cuz?"

Sarah raised her eyebrows. This was the first time since Tuesday that Tasha had spoken to her.

"That's right," Sarah responded. She leaned into her cousin. "Are you talking to me again?" she whispered.

"I'm over it," said Tasha. "If Julie O'Connor was going to spread that story about Billy, she would have done it by now."

56

When Jennifer appeared, she tossed her backpack in the middle of the table. "Tasha, look at this!" She gathered the fabric of her print skirt in her hands. Steve and José hooted as she raised her hem and exposed more of her tights. They stopped when all the girls gave them warning looks.

Jennifer pointed to the seam that ran up the side of the skirt. There was a four-inch rip in it. "I paid serious money for this skirt, and now it's coming apart."

"You're right, girl. Take it back," said Tasha. "Or I could sew it for you, and you'd never know it was there."

"No way," said Jennifer as she picked through the receipts in her purse. "They're going to give me my money back. They won't sell *me* trash like this."

Kwame tapped Jennifer's shoulder. "Excuse me."

Jennifer ignored him. "I've been walking around with a torn skirt all morning," she fumed. "I don't know who-all saw me like that."

"Jennifer?"

"Not now, Kwame, I'm not in a good mood."

"I was wondering if you could help *me* with *your* homework," said Kwame loudly. The others laughed, but Jennifer's glare was deadly.

"Kwame, we'll talk about this after school."

"We gotta talk now," said Kwame. "I've been doing too much of this diary project for you."

Jennifer put on her best hurt expression. "Weren't you the one who said this was a great project for a historian like you?"

"Yes, but—" Kwame began, but Jennifer's voice drowned him out.

"And didn't you say you would help me?"

"Help? Yes. Do all the work? No." He slid the diary across the table.

Jennifer bit her trembling lip. "I wish you'd told me that sooner," she said. "Because now half the diary will be in *your* handwriting and half in mine. What's Mrs. Parisi going to think?"

"All I know is—"

"She's going to think I cheated!" said Jennifer. "What am I going to do?"

Kwame looked for help from his friends. Tasha was about to speak up for him, but Sarah nudged her. "Let Kwame work his way out of this," she whispered. "He's got to learn to stand up to Jennifer."

But Kwame was no match for her. "I feel you're taking advantage of me," he said lamely.

"Don't try to explain, Kwame," said Jennifer irritably. "You want to back out of your promise? Go ahead."

"I'm not backing out of my promise."

"Then why don't you get together with me after school the way we've been doing?" said Jennifer.

"Because it hasn't worked!" said Kwame. "Every time we get together, you get on the phone and talk to your friends while I do everything."

"Can I help it if an emergency came up and I had to make some calls?" said Jennifer. She suddenly flashed him a smile. "Tonight we'll work on it, and I promise no distractions, okay?"

"Say no! Say no!" Sarah murmured.

"Okay," said Kwame.

Sarah and Tasha traded defeated looks.

"Is that her?" Tasha asked, pointing to a girl stand-ing by herself near the flagpole in front of Murphy High. They sat in the bus, waiting for the driver to close the door.

"No. Julie is over there," said Sarah, pointing to the main doors of the high school. Julie leaned against the building, looking lost in the large parka she had on.

"What is she staring at?" asked Tasha.

Sarah followed Julie's gaze and saw a group of boys who were throwing snowballs. It was not very smart, since a teacher could walk out the main doors any minute. But at least the boys had the sense to stay on the left side of the building, away from the vice-princi-pal's office. Mr. Schlesinger hated snowball fights. Sarah watched the boys. There seemed to be two sides, instead of just a free-for-all. She could make out Gary Iverson's thick, squat frame, and Bobby Olmos's brightly colored wool cap easily gave him away. Sarah saw a boy wearing a large red, black, and green patch on his jacket. It had to be Rashad Kamir, she realized. Rashad was from Nigeria, and he proudly wore the colors of Africa.

While Rashad tried to dodge a snowball from Bobby Olmos, Gary Iverson whipped one at his face from close range. Rashad only had time to turn so that it caught him on the side of the face.

"Ooh, I'll bet that hurt!" said Tasha near Sarah's ear.

When the bus rolled out of the parking lot, Sarah stole one last look at Julie. She was staring intently at Rashad, who had caught Gary and was wrestling with him.

Then it dawned on her. R is for Rashad! Julie's diary entries were about the Nigerian boy. He was certainly good-looking, and he was in Mrs. Parisi's history class.

It must be him, thought Sarah. She would know for sure tomorrow. Mrs. Parisi had announced a second worksheet, which meant trading diaries again. And Julie would probably mention the snowball fight.

Seven

That afternoon Cindy came over to do homework, but it was impossible to work in Sarah's room. Between Tasha's radio blaring and Allison and Pam's watching TV in Miss Essie's room, there were too many distractions.

"It's much quieter here," said Sarah, propping the door open with her foot to let Cindy into the kitchen. They dropped their books on the table and looked for a snack. They found a half-empty bag of potato chips and an unopened tub of onion dip.

"Let's get to it," said Cindy, opening her math book. She looked at Sarah, who was lost in thought. "Sarah?"

"Sorry. Where were we?"

Cindy laughed. "What's up with you today? Usually you're the one trying to get *me* to work."

"I was just thinking about that girl Julie O'Connor," said Sarah. "Do you know her?"

"Not that well," Cindy admitted. "I don't really like her." She saw the surprised look on Sarah's face. "I think she's a little stuck-up," she explained. "We sat in the same seat on the way back from that field trip to Colonial Williamsburg last year. In all those hours on the bus, she didn't say more than five words to me."

"She's not stuck-up; she's just terribly shy," said Sarah. Before she knew it, she found herself pouring out Julie's life story, from her demanding parents, to her eating obsession, to the mysterious "C" she took.

They were startled by the sound of the front door slamming. Hard. Sarah and Cindy went out and found Allison standing by the front door.

"Pam just left," said Allison, her face tense.

"You two have a fight?" said Sarah.

Allison didn't respond. She ran into the den and turned on the television.

"I was just trying to help," Sarah called after her.

After dinner, Sarah was surprised to hear her sister knocking on her door before entering. "Since when do you knock?" Sarah asked.

"Very funny," said Allison. She looked as if she'd been crying, and Sarah motioned her to a chair. Allison fidgeted for a few minutes before clearing her throat. "I've been going out with this guy," she said. "His name is Vaughn Cottrell."

Sarah nodded, and Allison continued.

"We go to his house after school. His dad has this real long race track for his electric cars right in the middle of the living room. Vaughn and I race them all the time. He beats me, but it's his set."

"What else do you do together?" Sarah asked gently.

"We go to the McDonald's near his house and he buys me chocolate shakes. He likes me a lot, and I like him, so . . ."

"So?"

"What do we do about kissing and stuff?"

"Have you already kissed?" Sarah asked, remembering the day they'd watched Vaughn kiss Allison. When Allison nodded, Sarah felt relieved. At least she's telling the truth, she thought.

"Have you gone any further?"

"No," said Allison. "That's what Eva and Giselle ask me in school. I like the kissing, but I don't want to do any more."

"Does Vaughn want you to?"

Allison shrugged. "Not really," she said. "He's kind of shy." She looked bewildered. "I've got a boyfriend, but I don't know what I'm *supposed* to be doing. How long do we just kiss before we go further?"

"How long? I don't know," said Sarah, suddenly wishing that Allison had taken her questions to their parents. "There are no official rules about things like that. But Mom once told me, 'When it comes to love and sex, don't do anything your best friend would be ashamed of.'"

Allison hesitated. "Pam?"

"Your best friend," said Sarah, "is Allison Gordon."

Allison smiled. "I'll remember that."

"And for heaven's sake, *never* do anything just because Eva and Giselle want you to."

"I know," said Allison impatiently. "We learned all about peer pressure in school. Eva and Giselle don't have boyfriends, so they want to know all the juicy details."

"When you get to high school, you'll notice only trashy people tell all the juicy details," said Sarah.

This seemed to satisfy Allison. "At least I'm not doing anything wrong," she said, heading for the door. "Thanks, Sarah."

"You're welcome!" Sarah called out after her.

When she was alone again, Sarah took a deep breath. Giving advice to her younger sister had made her feel good. And she was flattered Allison had confided in her.

But what if Allison didn't follow her advice? She thought of the boy, Vaughn Cottrell. What was he like? Would he try to go too far with her sister? Would he respect Allison? "If he doesn't, I'll kill him," Sarah murmured.

PINE

Eight

"You what?" said Jennifer in disbelief. It was Friday morning, and Kwame and Jennifer stood in the arts courtyard, an open area with benches and display cases full of students' artwork. Kwame looked sheepishly at his friend.

"I left your diary at home," he said.

"Kwame, how could you? We're supposed to trade them again today," said Jennifer.

"Don't blame me!" said Kwame. "If we had gone to your house like we agreed, none of this would have happened. You pulled the same disappearing act at my house that you did before."

Jennifer didn't reply. Instead, she opened her purse and rooted among the credit card slips until she found three crisp twenty-dollar bills. "There's still time," she said, handing Kwame one of the twenties. "Get a cab and pick up the diary."

"What!" said Kwame, backing away from the money. "I'll miss my math class," he said.

"I need that diary *today*," she said pleadingly.

Kwame took the chain with his house key from around his neck and handed it to her. "Look," he said. "I know you have a study period right before lunch, so why don't you get it?"

Jennifer took the key from Kwame's hand and sighed loudly. "Where is it?"

"In my bedroom, on the second shelf," said Kwame.

"It better be," said Jennifer. She hurried off just as Cindy was approaching them.

"What was that all about?" Cindy asked.

Kwame explained, and Cindy shook her head. "It's costing her more work to get out of her work than if she had done the work."

"I know," said Kwame. "I don't think Jennifer even reads what I help her write."

"Then why do you keep doing it?" said Cindy, falling in step with Kwame.

"I promised. And besides, I've learned a lot about Jennifer," he said.

"Like what?" said Cindy.

"I promised I wouldn't say," said Kwame. "But if I ever need money, I know who to blackmail!"

66

***

That afternoon Mrs. Parisi stood in front of the class with a pile of worksheets in her hand. "Today we'll switch diaries and look them over to study the relationships between people. List all the interactions you read about, and how the writer feels about them. Relationships between the writer and his or her parents, siblings, even pets. Did you all bring your diaries?" she asked. She pointed at Jennifer's empty desk. "I see we're missing someone."

She was here earlier today, thought Sarah. Where is she?

Dave, too, had noticed that Jennifer was missing. He caught Sarah looking at him and lifted his diary off the table.

He wants me to trade diaries with him, Sarah realized.

When the teacher finished handing out the new worksheet, she told everyone to trade. Sarah hurried to Julie's desk, not daring to look at Dave.

"I hope you like it," said Sarah.

"Me too," said Julie, handing hers over. Ever since they'd traded diaries Julie had acted more friendly to Sarah. It was odd, since Julie revealed so much about herself in her diary, but Sarah could help but wonder if it was a relief to Julie to pour her heart out.

Sarah returned to her desk and glanced at Dave. She expected him to look angry, but his expression was hard to read.

The classroom door opened, and Jennifer walked in.

67

She was still wearing her coat. "I'm sorry, Mrs. Parisi. I had an emergency," she said breathlessly, waving the diary in the air before handing it to Dave.

Sarah barely listened to the rest of the class. She was dying to open Julie's diary to find out what had happened over the past few days. She glanced at the worksheet on her desk and knew she would be busy that night. Julie's diary was all about relationships.

When the bell rang Sarah watched Julie dash out of the room. She'd been hoping to get a chance to talk with Julie, to draw her out some more. Sarah tried to follow her, but Dave stopped her.

"What's going on?" he said. "Why won't you trade diaries with me? Are you still mad about that stupid party?"

"I'll be honest, Dave," said Sarah. "When I first started, I didn't know we were going to trade them. I was very honest about everybody. Too honest!"

"There must be some stuff about me you don't want me to read."

"Dave, I swear that I didn't write anything bad about you. In fact, the stuff I wrote is too good!" said Sarah.

He gave her a surprised look. "Uh, huh."

."Are you still mad at me?" Sarah asked.

"I'll get over it," he said.

Sarah stood on her toes and gave him a quick kiss on the cheek. Dave put his arms around her and returned the kiss.

They were startled by a scream, then shouts from

68

several students. Dave and Sarah ran toward the crowd gathering ahead of them in the hallway. At first, Sarah thought it might be a fight. When they arrived, however, she was stunned to find Julie O'Connor crumpled on the floor.

Nine

"Let me through," shouted Sarah, pushing her way into the group of students.

"Give her some air, man," Dave said, spreading his arms and pushing the crowd back.

When Sarah reached Julie, the other girl seemed to be regaining consciousness. "Are you okay?" Sarah asked, lifting Julie's head.

"What happened?" Julie said in a weak voice.

"Looks like you fainted again," Sarah told her.

"Somebody call an ambulance," shouted a student.

Julie sat up quickly, then steadied herself by placing her hands on the floor. "I don't need an ambulance," she said. "I'll be all right."

"Let's have the nurse take a look at you," said Dave.

But Julie shook her head. "I'm fine," she insisted. "I just need something to eat, that's all." She got all the way to her feet and Dave handed over her backpack.

Sarah gave Dave a grateful look, then guided Julie to the nearest girls' bathroom. "We have to talk," she said once they were inside. "And don't tell me you're 'fine,' because I know you're not." She heard the tardy bell ring.

"Don't you have a class to go to?" Julie asked sullenly.

"If you don't want to talk to me, you can talk to the nurse," said Sarah. "Because that's where I'll go right after this."

Julie sighed and set her backpack on the sink. She unzipped the front pocket and pulled out a rice cake wrapped in plastic. Sarah pointed to it. "Is that the first thing you've eaten today?"

"Of course not," said Julie.

Sarah wasn't convinced. "Look, I know you're trying to punish your parents by not eating," she said. "But you're just punishing yourself."

"I'm handling it."

"How? By fainting in the middle of the hallway?" Sarah shot back. "I read your diary, remember? I know you're under a lot of pressure, but starving yourself, and taking cocaine—"

"Cocaine?"

"What does the 'C' in your diary stand for?" asked

Sarah. "Isn't it cocaine?"

Julie laughed. From her pocket, she pulled out a red and white box with the words "Sleepaway Caffeine Tabs." "Straight from the drugstore," Julie said dryly.

Sarah shrugged. "Okay, so it's not cocaine—but it's still a drug. Face it, Julie, something is wrong. You've fainted twice in the past week. And," she added grimly, "it sounds like you've got problems at home. You can't go on like this."

"Well, what do you want me to do?" Julie said. Tears brimmed in her eyes.

"Let's go talk to a guidance counselor," said Sarah softly.

"No!" said Julie through clenched teeth. "I'm not going to talk to any counselors. Next thing I know, they're calling my parents in for a conference. That's the last thing I need." She zipped up her backpack and headed for the door.

"If you don't do something, I will," Sarah called out after her.

Julie didn't reply.

That evening Sarah read the latest entries in Julie's diary. It seemed Julie had started writing the minute she had gotten her own diary back. Sarah had hoped the situation at the O'Connor home had improved, but if anything, it had gotten worse.

Wednesday
Only 30 calories on Tuesday! Those C pills are

73

doing the trick, even though I didn't get much sleep.

Last night, I found Dad looking in my room for my test grades (and other stuff, probably). He gave me the same line about not having secrets in his household. He said he knew what was going on every night at dinner, and that I was immature for trying to get attention by not eating. Whatever you say, Dad. But tell me this: How am I supposed to keep my grades up if I have to watch Lettie all afternoon? I asked Mom about getting the baby-sitter to watch her even on the days I don't have a lesson, but she turned it around and started asking me why I wanted the free time, all of a sudden. Was I doing something they should know about? She actually asked me if I was trying drugs.

To top it off, my voice cracked a lot during my lesson. Mr. Hannes said he could tell I hadn't done the vocal drills he gave me.

Thursday
R. got hit in the face with a snowball! I saw him on the bus later, and his cheek was all swollen. I asked him about it, even though I saw the whole thing. At least it was a chance to talk to him.

Sarah smiled. Rashad was indeed the "R" in Julie's diary. Just as I guessed, she thought. It was a good thing Julie had a crush on someone. Besides her older brother in Kentucky, whom she'd called once or twice, Rashad was the only positive glimmer in Julie's latest entries.

Lettie wanted me to fingerpaint with her, and I got mad when she wouldn't stop asking me. I yelled at her, and she started crying. I still feel like dirt. (Later) Mom just left the room. She came in to ask what was wrong with me lately, and I started crying. What should I say, "everything"? She was worried sick, but I couldn't tell her anything about me. I don't even know what's going on myself.

It was hard to believe the same Julie who was always so quiet in school was seething with frustration at home. Sarah was also amazed that Julie continued to write so honestly when she knew Sarah would be reading her journal.

But as Sarah began to close the journal, she noticed something that she clearly wasn't supposed to see. At the bottom of the page were a few words Julie had written, then crossed out with another pen. Sarah stared at the page, trying to read what the other girl had written. Finally she made out the words: *It all ends Wednesday.*

Ten

Sarah brooded about Julie's crossed-out sentence the entire weekend. Could Julie actually be considering suicide? she wondered. Sarah had never known anyone who had actually committed suicide, but her father had told Sarah and Tasha about a boy at Hamilton High who had tried to kill himself the year before. He was in counseling now, but the attempt had sent a jolt through the entire high school.

Sarah wanted to call Julie and ask her about her entry, but she felt awkward, especially when she remembered how angry Julie had looked on Friday, when they had talked in the bathroom.

77

By Sunday afternoon, Sarah couldn't resist any longer. She called four O'Connor families before reaching the right one. Julie sounded surprised by the call.

"If this is about last Friday—" Julie began.

"No, I was just wondering if you liked my diary," Sarah said as cheerfully as possible.

"Yes," said Julie cautiously. "It's good—especially the part about you and your cousin. Also the part about Jennifer was very funny."

"Thanks," said Sarah. "Yours is...uh, fascinating. I couldn't put it down."

"Yes, well, I was thinking about calling you," said Julie hastily. "I think I got a little overdramatic. I guess I complain a lot, and make things sound worse than they are."

"I don't think you complain a lot," said Sarah. "From what I've read, you've got a lot on your mind." In the background, Sarah heard a girl's voice calling for Julie. "Is that your sister?"

"Yes, and she wants to fingerpaint," said Julie. She covered the phone and said something to Lettie that seemed to quiet her down. "I've got a few minutes while Lettie changes her shirt."

"She sounds like a real handful," said Sarah.

"She is," said Julie. She began to describe the things Lettie liked to do.

Sarah listened and quickly sensed that Julie would rather talk about Lettie than about herself. When Lettie returned, Julie said good-bye and hung up. Sarah sighed. She didn't know any more about Julie's mysterious crossed-out sentence than she had before.

A shout erupted from down the hall. From the phone stand in the hallway Sarah saw Allison's friend Pam running down the stairs in tears. She grabbed her coat and boots, and then left, slamming the door.

"Not again," said Tasha, coming out of her room and joining her cousin at the banister.

They watched as Allison ran down the stairs and opened the front door again. "Don't come back!" Allison shouted. She shut the door hard and ran into the den.

"Who keeps banging the front door?" said Mr. Gordon, coming up from his workshop in the basement. He had on his safety goggles, and his face was smudged with sawdust. He saw the older girls at the top of the staircase and glared at them.

"It wasn't us," Sarah and Tasha chorused. Mr. Gordon stormed into the den. A minute later, they heard the television go off.

"What is it with Allison and Pam these days?" said Tasha, following Sarah into her room.

"I don't know," said Sarah, wondering if it had anything to do with Allison's boyfriend.

"What was that talk you and Allison had last week?" asked Tasha.

"Just some questions she had," said Sarah.

"Anything I need to know?"

"Actually, I promised not to tell," said Sarah.

"Is it about that boy we caught her with?" said

79

Tasha with a mischievous grin.

"I can't say, cuz," said Sarah.

Allison knocked on Sarah's door, then walked in. "Can you excuse us for a minute, Tasha?" she asked. Once Tasha had left, Allison climbed onto Sarah's bed.

"Shoes off," Sarah ordered. Allison removed them. "Is Pam mad at you again?"

Allison nodded. "She is so immature! We're going to the Madison Orchestra concert on a field trip this Thursday, and Pam 'reserved' the seat next to me on the bus."

Sarah laughed softly. "Let me guess: Vaughn wants to sit next to you, right?"

"Yeah."

"Did you already promise Pam the seat?" said Sarah. She saw the sheepish look on her younger sister's face and immediately knew the answer to her question. "No wonder she's mad. You broke your promise to her."

"Still, she's blowing it all out of proportion," said Allison. "It's just a stupid bus ride downtown."

"It meant a lot to Pam," Sarah pointed out.

"I know," said Allison. "Maybe I should call Pam and tell her it's hers again. Of course, then I have to call Vaughn and tell him he can't have it."

"You'll work something out," said Sarah. "If the two of you made up from Thursday's fight, you can make up after this one."

Allison shook her head. "I don't think so. The reason we made up last time was because I promised she

80

could sit next to me on the field trip bus!"

"Oh." Sarah didn't know what else to say.

"What am I going to do?"

"Look, Allison, sometimes it's hard to juggle a boy-friend with your other friends. Being with Vaughn is taking up the time you used to spend with Pam. No wonder she's upset. She's probably a little lonely, too." Sarah wasn't sure Allison was even paying attention. She had a faraway look in her eyes.

"I'll think of something," Allison said a few seconds later.

After Allison had gone, Sarah let out a sigh. She didn't know how to handle Julie's problems, and now she had let down Allison, too.

Later that night, Sarah knocked on the bathroom door.

"It's open," Tasha called out. Sarah opened the door and found her cousin combing her shoulder-length hair over the sink.

Tasha looked at her cousin and frowned. "I'll be out in a minute," she said.

"You're mad at me," said Sarah. "What's wrong?"

"Why should I tell you? You don't tell me anything anymore."

"You mean about Allison?"

"And Julie, too. She passed out in the middle of the hallway on Friday, and Dave said you talked with her. What's going on?" said Tasha.

"I would never tell *anyone* about Julie," said Sarah.

"That's private."

"You told Cindy," Tasha reminded her. "When the two of you were doing homework in the kitchen."

Sarah suddenly remembered. "Cindy thought Julie was stuck-up," she said. "I just wanted to prove she wasn't. And what were you doing eavesdropping on our conversation?"

"It's the only way I learn anything around here," said Tasha hotly. "I told you what happened to me and Billy last week, but you don't trust me with what you know."

Sarah locked the bathroom door and sat on the edge of the tub. "Allison and I have been talking about Vaughn—" she began.

Afterward Sarah returned to her room and began to fill her backpack with her textbooks for the next day. She felt a twinge of guilt for betraying Allison's trust. But it's more important that Tasha not feel left out of things, she told herself. Even though her cousin was happy living with the Gordons, Sarah knew there were times when Tasha still felt like an outsider.

Then Sarah noticed that the diary wasn't on her nightstand. She looked on her desk, then glanced in her bookbag. Finally she looked under the telephone stand in the hallway where she had talked to Julie.

The diary was gone.

She strode to Allison's room and opened the door, but Allison wasn't there. Her room was a mess of jumbled bedding, dirty clothes, and dolls. Sarah looked in Allison's closet and under the bed, but found nothing.

As she was checking the shower in her parents' bathroom, Sarah began to feel foolish. Maybe I misplaced it, she thought.

She heard a noise upstairs and headed for the stairway that led to the attic. Through the crack at the bottom of the attic door, the light from the bare bulb shone through. Making as little noise as possible, Sarah climbed up the stairs. When she tried to turn the door handle, she found it locked.

"Allison?"

Allison didn't answer.

"Open this door right now!" Sarah warned.

"Promise you won't be mad," said Allison.

"I won't promise a thing," said Sarah hotly. "Is this the way you pay me back for helping you?"

"I didn't take it from your room," said Allison. "I found it by the telephone in the hallway. And besides, it's not even your diary. It's another girl's, and boy does she have problems."

Sarah pounded on the attic door. "It's none of your business whose it is. Open this door now!"

Miss Essie heard the pounding and appeared at the bottom of the attic stairs. "What is going on? Come out of the attic, Allison," she said, climbing to where Sarah stood.

Sarah heard other voices below and turned to see her mother and father right behind her.

"What is going on?" asked Mrs. Gordon. She was dressed in a pair of old exercise pants and a T-shirt and carrying some legal papers.

"Allison took my diary," said Sarah.

"Is that any reason to shout?" said Mr. Gordon.

"Let me in," said Miss Essie through the attic door. Allison opened it, and Sarah and Mr. and Mrs. Gordon backed down the staircase as Miss Essie ushered Allison down.

Sarah's mother gave her a weary look. "Don't you think you're a little old to be chasing your sister?" she said.

"You don't know what she did," said Sarah. She began to explain, but she sensed that her mother was eager to finish her work. Sarah mumbled a quick apology and bit her lip in frustration as she watched her parents go back downstairs.

They didn't even give me a chance to explain, Sarah thought angrily. It dawned on her that this was how Julie felt about her parents all the time.

PINE

Eleven

Miss Essie liked to sleep late, so Sarah was surprised to find her grandmother up when she walked into the kitchen on Monday morning. "You've been busy," Sarah said, lifting the lid that covered the dish of scrambled eggs. Another plate held thick slices of sausage.

"Eat," said Miss Essie. She made a face when Sarah took only a small helping of eggs and one sausage patty. "Is that all you're going to have? You'll pass out before ten o'clock."

Sarah shook her head. "This is plenty," she said. It might not be as much food as Miss Essie liked to see her eat, but it was surely more than Julie had eaten on the days she had passed out. Still, Sarah allowed Miss Essie to pile another helping of scrambled eggs onto her plate.

"I'll have more, too, Grandma," said Allison. She was up earlier than usual as well. She gave Sarah a tentative smile, and Sarah scowled back at her.

"Did you forget something, girl?" said Miss Essie. "What did we talk about last night?"

"I'm sorry about last night," said Allison, turning to Sarah. She looked as though she wanted to stop there, but Miss Essie's stern expression made her go on. "And I want to make it up to you," said Allison. The words sounded rehearsed. "Tonight I'll put away the dishes and clean the kitchen, even though it's your turn."

"In that case, I accept your apology," said Sarah. She smiled at Allison, feeling a little guilty again that she had told Tasha about her sister's troubles. Oh well, Sarah thought, maybe I'll help her with the dishes after dinner.

When Tasha came down to breakfast, it was almost time to be at the bus stop. Tasha had on a gray wool sweater that would have cost a fortune, if she hadn't made it herself, and the black wool pants matched it perfectly. She had put on some of her best jewelry.

"We're going to school, girl, not the White House," Sarah joked.

"Just want to look good," said Tasha. "When I look good, I feel good."

86

"Well, then you ought to be feeling great," said Sarah admiringly.

At school, Sarah immediately went looking for Julie, but she wasn't at her locker. And later there was no sign of her in the cafeteria. Did Julie spend lunchtime in the library? Sarah wondered.

"Is this seat taken?" Dave nudged Sarah with his hip as he set his tray down. Before Sarah could reply, Robert Thornton approached Dave.

"There's a pickup game at the gym starting up right now," said Robert, making a jump-shot motion with his hands. "We need your legs, man."

Dave stood up to go, and Sarah pointed at the uneaten lunch on the tray. "Aren't you going to eat?"

"I'll pick up some food from the senior snack bar in the activities lounge later," said Dave. He followed Robert out of the cafeteria to the gymnasium.

When Kwame saw the abandoned lunch tray, he broke into a wide smile. "This is the first good thing that's happened to me all day," he declared.

"You're in the school cafeteria," Sarah reminded him. "The food is not exactly anything to get excited about."

Jennifer suddenly appeared behind Kwame. "Did you bring Dave's diary?" she asked him.

"It's in the backpack," said Kwame through a mouthful of spaghetti. He pulled out Dave's diary and handed it to Jennifer. "This is the last time I'm doing your homework," he said firmly. "I have too much else to do without doing your work, too."

"Did you hear that?" Jennifer told the table. "Mrs. Parisi is going to see the different handwritings and think I cheated."

"But you did," said Kwame.

"If she thinks I cheated, she'll kick me out," said Jennifer. "Is that what you want her to do?"

"Try to do your own entries in my handwriting," said Kwame. "Because I waited for you to come over all weekend, and you never showed up."

"My mother had to go to New York City on business, and she had enough frequent flyer miles to take me along," said Jennifer hotly. "Did you expect me to pass up a chance to go to New York City over the weekend? With my mother? Besides, Kwame, you *owe* me after making me spend almost a whole afternoon looking for that diary in your house."

"I don't owe you a thing," said Kwame.

Jennifer glared at him, then grabbed her bookbag and left the table. Kwame looked at Dave's tray and slowly pushed it away.

"Don't tell me she upset you with that," said Cindy.

"I know I'm doing the right thing," Kwame explained, "but I still feel like I broke a promise."

"You *are* doing the right thing, and don't feel bad," said Tasha. "If Jennifer doesn't like this project, that's too darn bad. Everyone else in her class has found a way to do it."

"I guess you're right," said Kwame. "Women are my weakness."

"I hear you," said Billy, nodding in agreement.

Tasha nudged him. "Hey, José," he called out when José, Steve, and April arrived. "How's the great kitten giveaway?"

José looked at him glumly. "We still have three," he announced. "I'm sick of trying."

"Maybe we should try putting an ad on my bulletin board at home," said Steve. "It's a computer bulletin board," he explained. "They have a screen for announcements, personal messages and stuff."

"At this point, I'll try anything," José said.

"I was just in the girls' room a minute ago," April told Cindy as she sat down, "and I saw Jennifer crying. What's going on?"

When Kwame heard this, he sighed loudly, gathered his books, and walked in the direction April had pointed in.

"Is he heading for the girls' bathroom?" Tasha whispered as they watched him.

"Nice going, April," said Cindy. She explained the argument their friend had missed moments before.

April watched Kwame disappear through the cafeteria doors. "You don't think Kwame is going to apologize, do you?"

"Not just apologize, but also offer to do the assignment for her tonight," Sarah predicted.

When Sarah had finished eating she stood up and said good-bye to her friends. "I'm going to check out the library."

Sarah quickly found Julie sitting in a carrel, lost in a book. "What are you reading?" asked Sarah.

89

Julie looked up, startled. She held up the book. It was *I Know Why the Caged Bird Sings,* by Maya Angelou.

"Great book," said Sarah, sitting next to her.

"It's one of my favorites."

"Look, Julie, I meant to ask you more about your diary last night before Lettie cut us off," said Sarah quickly. "You sounded pretty upset in the last entry. And you really scared me when you fainted again on Friday."

Julie shook her head. "The diary is just a way to blow off steam," she said casually. "It's not as bad as I said it was. I'm really fine."

"I don't believe that, and neither do you. You *wanted* someone to know what was going on at home, or you wouldn't have written it in here," said Sarah, pointing to the notebook. "I want to help you. It's hard for me to stand by, knowing you popped caffeine pills and were trying to starve yourself."

"I'm not starving myself!" said Julie.

"You wrote in your diary that you only ate thirty calories last Tuesday. That's two Life Savers!" said Sarah. "I thought we could work something out, but since you don't want to talk about it, I'm going to go to your guidance counselor and tell her everything."

Julie grabbed her arm. "I'll talk to you all you want. It won't do any good, but I'll do it."

"When?"

"After my music lesson today," said Julie, returning to her book.

In history class, Mrs. Parisi collected the second set of worksheets and told everyone to get their diaries back. "I'll hand out the final worksheet on Wednesday," she announced.

Maybe that's what Julie had meant when she said it would all end Wednesday, Sarah thought. But how could she have known that was what Mrs. Parisi had in mind? And why would Julie bother to cross it out?

After her last class Sarah made her way to Julie's bus. She found Julie sitting near the front, her face already buried in her Maya Angelou book. Amanda Dennis were sitting nearby. She gave Sarah a hostile look, as if the bus were her private car and Sarah had entered uninvited. The last thing Sarah wanted was to have one of the pep squad girls overhearing Julie's troubles, so she made her way to a seat in the back where Rashad was sitting with his friends.

"Hey, Sarah Gordon, you got on the wrong bus," said Rashad. His English had a strong Nigerian accent.

"The bus driver's paying me to keep an eye on you," said Sarah. Rashad laughed. He still had a slight swelling on his cheek from the snowball.

When the bus stopped in front of the Madison Arts Guild, Julie got out, and Sarah followed her. "We can talk after my lesson," said Julie as they walked through the brass doors. Sarah glanced at the wide hallway. The first door led to a reception area, but the others seemed to be rehearsal rooms. A sign advertised a drawing class on the third floor of the building. From the basement, she heard someone practicing scales on a trumpet.

A man appeared from one of the rehearsal rooms. He was short, with blond hair and a thick beard. He smiled at Sarah and motioned Julie into his room. Sarah knew this was Mr. Hannes.

"If you would like to wait for Julie, there is a rehearsal room next door that is empty at this hour," he told Sarah.

There was a piano in the empty room, and Sarah sat on the stool, putting her homework on the music stand in front of her. She could hear Julie's voice faintly coming into the room. Sarah wished she could hear better. It sounded as if Julie had a beautiful voice.

Halfway through the lesson, Julie knocked on the door where Sarah was waiting. "I didn't know if you were still here," she said.

"I'm not going anywhere," replied Sarah.

When Julie's lesson had finally ended, she gathered her books and met the other girl in the hallway, and they walked out to the bus stop.

"You have a beautiful voice," said Sarah. "How did the lesson go?"

Julie shrugged. "My teacher said my voice control had improved."

"You don't seem too happy about it."

"I think that was my last lesson," said Julie, looking straight ahead.

"You're quitting?" Sarah asked in disbelief.

"I don't have time for them," said Julie. "You see

how I'm rushing to lessons, rushing home, then at night I'm rushing to do my work for school. It's not worth it."

Her voice sounded dull and flat; as if all the life had gone from it.

"Uh, Julie," Sarah began, "I saw the sentence you tried to scribble out of your diary. I...I'm afraid you're planning to do something drastic."

Julie whirled toward her. "You don't know what you're talking about," she said in a voice so cold and angry, it startled Sarah. Julie waved at the approaching bus with both hands.

"Julie, you promised to talk to me," Sarah said softly.

"I will. Tomorrow. But not about that!" said Julie. She got into the bus. The doors closed before Sarah could decide whether to follow her.

Sarah ran to a pay phone and dialed the O'Connor home. She hated to go behind Julie's back, but she didn't know what else to do. Julie was very depressed, and her parents should know how serious the situation was. Besides, they couldn't let her give up her voice lessons—they were the one thing Julie did that was just for her.

The woman who baby-sat while Julie was at her voice lesson answered the phone. Sarah left a message to have Julie's parents call her at home.

As soon as Sarah stepped through the door she asked if there were any messages for her.

"None," Mrs. Gordon called out.

Sarah called the O'Connors again, but this time Julie answered.

"I found the message you left for my parents, Sarah," Julie said, "and I ripped it up. Don't you dare bring them into this!" Then she slammed down the receiver.

Twelve

"Why don't we just use his computer here?" said José, pointing to the system in Mr. Adams's home office.

Steve finished disconnecting his father's modem. "I'm not supposed to use his computer. I put an infected disk into his system last year." He explained about the computer virus known as The Groundhog. On February 2, Groundhog Day, the virus had created havoc with his father's files.

Back in his room, Steve connected the modem and logged on to COMICAZI, a computer network for comic-book buffs.

"Cool," said José, his face lit up by the screen. He

heard a faint meow and turned to find Kirby entering the room, his tail held high. "We're trying to find homes for your brothers and sisters," he told the kitten.

Steve found the Buy/Trade section and invited José to sit down at the keyboard. "Type your advertisement in that box, and that's it."

Beautiful purebred kittens, José typed.

"Whoa, José. You can't use the word 'purebred' in there," said Kwame. "They're not Siamese, or Manx or anything."

"I didn't say they were. I said they were purebred kittens," said José. "They don't have any dog in them."

Fifteen minutes later, José was satisfied:

Beautiful purebred kittens available to good homes. Hurry! Only 3 left. Save them from the animal shelter!

"Type your phone number and your area code," said Steve. "This network has subscribers all over the country." He guided José through all the directories in the COMICAZI system. They read fan letters, articles, and reviews. "What's this one?" said José, guiding the mouse to the heading "Troya."

Steve grinned. "Why don't you see for yourself?"

José clicked the button, and Steve's computer screen went blank. Then, slowly, a drawing unscrolled on the screen. It was a picture of the comic-book character Troya in a very skimpy bathing suit.

"Wow!" said Kwame and José.

"*That's* why I need a color monitor," said Steve.

Suddenly a different girl intruded into Kwame's mind. "Dang! I have to go," he said. "I have to meet

96

Jennifer at her house in ten minutes so we can do her diary thing," he explained. He hurried up the basement stairs.

"She's leading you around by the nose, man," said José.

"I know," said Kwame. "But every time I try to get out of it, she flips out. What really bothers me is that I don't think she looks over what I write."

Suddenly Steve grinned. "Why don't you find out?" he said. Kwame gave him a quizzical look. "Write something different in the diary and see if she catches it."

"That's dishonest," said Kwame. "And sneaky, too." His friend just grinned. Kwame grinned back. He removed his coat and pulled the diary from his backpack. "Let's get started," he said.

PINE

Thirteen

At school the next day Sarah found Julie at Julie's locker. To Sarah's surprise, Julie smiled when Sarah approached.

"Before you say anything," Julie said, "I want to apologize for what I said on the phone and what happened at the bus stop yesterday. I freaked out."

"That's okay," Sarah said.

Julie's face got tense. "Listen, Sarah, have you been telling all your friends about my diary? I don't want a lot of people knowing what's going on in my life."

"Of course not!" said Sarah. "Did you tell anyone what I wrote in mine?" She was shocked to see Julie

99

nod.

"My sister, Lettie," said Julie, smiling. "She wanted to know what was making me laugh."

Sarah spied a picture of a boy taped to the inside of Julie's locker door. The boy had a broad smile and a handsome face that looked a little like Julie's. "Is that your brother, Brian?" asked Sarah. Julie nodded. "He's cute."

"He got all the good looks," said Julie ruefully.

"That's what I think about with my cousin sometimes," said Sarah. She was surprised to hear herself say it.

"You're just trying to make me feel better," said Julie.

"No, it's true. If you want to feel invisible, walk next to Tasha when there are lots of boys around!" said Sarah.

Julie laughed. "I feel invisible all the time," she said as her smile faded away.

"You don't have to be," said Sarah. She pointed to the diary in Julie's locker. "When you write, you have personality, humor, sensitivity. All you have to do is get it off the page and onto you."

"What good is all that when you look like me?" said Julie.

"Your looks are the easiest thing to work on," said Sarah. "We could start with your hair."

"Hey, you two. What's up?" said Cindy, approaching them. Julie immediately turned to rummage in her locker. Cindy raised one eyebrow at Sarah.

"Remember me, Julie?" Cindy asked. "I rode back from Colonial Williamsburg with you."

"You kept cracking up those girls in the seat in front of us," said Julie.

"That's right." Cindy beamed.

"We were just talking about Julie's getting her hair done," Sarah told her friend. She pointed to Cindy proudly and told Julie, "She's the best in the school."

"Maybe someday," said Julie. "Right now, I'd better get to homeroom."

"Wait," said Sarah, catching up. She motioned for Cindy to stay back. "Do you want to get together this afternoon?"

"You know I have to be with Lettie," Julie said.

"Maybe Cindy and I could come over. Lettie would have two more playmates, and we could do your hair," said Sarah. Julie looked doubtful. "Even if you don't get your hair done, we could distract Lettie while you did homework or something."

"Can I think about it?" said Julie.

"Think about it, then say yes," Sarah replied firmly.

It took a lot of persuading at lunchtime for Julie to finally say yes. After school Sarah ran to Julie's locker to make sure she didn't disappear again. They met Cindy at the main doors, and the three of them boarded the school bus to Julie's house. It turned out to be the same one that she took to her voice lesson, and Sarah waved to Rashad when he saw her again.

"Got on the wrong bus again?" he teased.

"We came to see you," Sarah teased back.

Rashad beamed. "Happens all the time," he declared.

Sarah and Cindy laughed, but Julie was desperately trying to get back to the safety of the front of the bus. She kept her eyes firmly on her shoes.

As they were picking up the permanent kit in the drugstore, Julie told Sarah and Cindy what to expect at her house. "Lettie is very affectionate," she told them. "So don't be surprised if she comes up and gives you a hug." From the drugstore they walked two blocks to a neighborhood of white brick houses with small yards bordered by chain-link fences. Julie walked up to one of the doors and rang the doorbell.

"Lettie loves to answer the door and see me there," Julie explained.

Lettie opened the door and squealed, "Julie!" She grabbed her older sister around the waist and hugged her tightly. Lettie was short and wide around the middle. The hands that clasped the waist of her older sister were thick, and her fingers were small and stubby. When Julie finally pulled away, Sarah saw Lettie's slightly angled eyes looking at her with curiosity.

"Lettie, say hello to Sarah," said Julie, pointing.

Lettie gave Sarah a shy hello.

"And this is Cindy."

The baby-sitter looked surprised to see Julie coming in with other people. She talked to Julie for a few minutes, then left.

"Hey, Lettie, is this your ball?" said Cindy, picking

up an inflated beach ball. Lettie opened her arms to catch it, and Cindy threw it to her. They played this way for a few minutes.

"She'll play catch with you all day if you let her," Julie warned.

"That's okay," said Cindy, tossing the ball. It was Lettie who stopped the game. She rushed up to Cindy and gave her a big hug.

After Julie had moved the kitchen table out of the way and cleared the sink of dishes, Cindy had Julie sit down while she spread Vaseline around her hairline. The Vaseline prevented the perm from stinging the exposed skin.

Lettie began to cry, and Sarah appeared at the kitchen doorway. "I think she wants to be in the same room with you," she told Julie.

"We can't have her here," said Cindy. "I'm afraid she might touch the straightener. That stuff stings."

Lettie wriggled past Sarah and gave Julie another hug. "Here, Lettie," said Julie, pulling a second chair toward the sink. "Sit next to me." The sight of the sisters sitting together gave Cindy an idea.

"Why don't we give Lettie a perm, too?" she said.

"I don't know," said Julie slowly. "What if we get some of the gel on her skin? She won't know what's going on, and she'll panic."

"She won't get any on her skin," Cindy assured Julie, "because I'll do her hair, and Sarah can do yours."

"Wait a minute, girlfriend!" said Sarah quickly.

103

"You're the expert here, not me."

"It's simple," Cindy insisted. "There's only four steps to it: perm, deactivating shampoo, regular shampoo, and conditioner." She turned to Julie. "You have any more money?"

"Mom and Dad always leave some emergency money," said Julie.

Cindy pointed to Lettie's hair. "This is an emergency!"

Sarah ran to the drugstore for another permanent kit. When she returned, Cindy had finished spreading the Vaseline around Lettie's hairline. She had also combed the hair of both girls into four separate areas.

"We start in the back," said Cindy, putting on the plastic gloves that came with the kit. She dipped her hand in the white gel and carefully spread it on a lock of Lettie's hair. At first Lettie fidgeted, but when she saw Sarah doing the same thing to Julie's hair, she puffed up with pride. The only time Lettie cried was after the perm, when Cindy was styling her hair and accidentally got too close with the blow-dryer.

"You look great!" said Sarah. Julie was turning from side to side in front of the bathroom mirror.

Julie could not get over the difference it made.

"Come here and look at your sister!" Cindy called out from Julie's bedroom. They found Lettie at the edge of Julie's bed. Lettie's short hair was styled close to her scalp, combed away from her face on the sides, and curled on the top.

"Just like Julie," said Lettie. She gave Cindy a big

smile.

It was getting dark when Cindy and Sarah finally left for home. Julie and Lettie waved to them from the open door. "Thanks for everything," said Julie.

"That Lettie is a handful," said Cindy as they rode the city bus across town.

"I noticed," said Sarah. "Julie loves her, but the trouble is, she has to take care of Lettie every day. No wonder she's down all the time."

"She didn't look down when you finished doing her hair," said Cindy. "Maybe if she looks better, she'll feel better about herself."

"I hope so," said Sarah. "But she needs friends to bring her out of her shell. She spends all her time alone—escaping from things."

Cindy shook her head. "Maybe, but it's easier to change a hairdo than a personality."

"She's got a great personality. I just wish she would bring it out," said Sarah.

The first person Sarah saw when she walked into her house that evening was Vaughn. He was talking to someone on the telephone in the den, and Sarah waved to him when he peeked out.

"Let's go, Vaughn," said Allison from inside the den. "It's already set up."

Vaughn quickly hung up and hurried to Allison.

Sarah found her mother in the kitchen, looking at the meat thermometer, which was stuck into one of a pair of roasting chickens on the counter. "You're just in time," said Mrs. Gordon. She motioned for Sarah to open the oven door so she could put the chickens back in. "Could you go to the den and ask Allison's friend if he's called his mother?"

"He did," said Sarah. She picked up a stack of dishes and headed to the dining room with them. From the den she heard the noise of a fierce video battle.

"Go for the fighter! Use one of your stun bolts," Allison commanded.

"I'm trying!" cried Vaughn after Allison's ninth suggestion.

At the dinner table, Allison told Vaughn where to sit. When he refused Miss Essie's lima beans, Allison persuaded him to take a small helping. After dinner they returned to the den to wait for Vaughn's mother to take him home. They argued over which video game to play, and Allison won out.

"She drives that boy like a car," Miss Essie announced in the kitchen.

Mr. Gordon turned from the sink and pointed to the apron he wore. "It's good for him," he said with a wink. "It will prepare him for marriage."

"I heard that, Uncle Donald," said Tasha as she walked in with the last of the dirty plates. "Do you think all women are bossy?"

Mr. Gordon looked at the four women in the room, who were waiting for him to answer. He chose his words carefully. "No."

"Allison *has* been a little pushy with him," Mrs. Gordon admitted.

"If that was a push, I'd hate to see a shove!" muttered Miss Essie. They all laughed.

Sarah was alone in the kitchen when Vaughn finally left. She leaned the broom against the doorway and peeked out to watch him put on his coat.

Allison was right behind him. "Don't run! It's slippery," she called out from the doorway. Sarah couldn't see him, but she was sure Vaughn walked the rest of the way.

"What do you think of Vaughn?" Allison asked Sarah eagerly.

"He's cute. And he's very polite," Sarah began.

"Yeah. Vaughn is a lot more fun than Pam," said Allison.

"It doesn't have to be a choice between the two of them," said Sarah, pointing the dustpan at her sister. "They can both be friends."

"Impossible," Allison replied. "Pam hates him."

"That's because you spend all your time with him."

"I like to be with him," said Allison simply.

Sarah followed her sister into the den. "That's because you can boss him around. That boy does everything you tell him."

Allison turned on the television and sat down. "You don't hear him complaining," she said.

PINE

Fourteen

Sarah had worried about what would happen on Wednesday ever since she had discovered Julie's ominous note to herself. She'd felt a lot better during the perm session the previous afternoon, when Julie had come out of her shell. Julie had chatted about school with Cindy and Sarah as if they had been friends for years. It made Sarah feel more confident about her.

But Wednesday morning when Sarah and Tasha saw Julie at her locker, Sarah's optimism faded. The shy girl had combed out the careful styling and tied her hair into the usual ponytail. Worse still, Julie's eyes were red and puffy, as if she'd been crying.

109

"Julie, what's up?" said Sarah.

"Nothing much," said Julie. She touched her ponytail and looked at Sarah apologetically. "Thanks for coming over yesterday. I... I didn't have time to style it this morning."

"What did your parents think about Lettie's new 'do'?" Sarah asked.

Julie's eyes filled with tears. "They liked it fine," she whispered.

"What's up with her?" Tasha asked, as Julie hurried away from them.

"I don't know," said Sarah. The homeroom bell rang before she could find out.

Julie was not in the library during lunch that afternoon. Sarah looked in the cafeteria and the gymnasium but did not find her there, either. Finally she spotted Julie by the pay phones near the main office. She was speaking in low tones and scribbling something on the walls of the booth. The minute Julie saw Sarah, she hung up and hastily rubbed at whatever she'd written down.

"Something's wrong, Julie. What is it?" Sarah asked.

"Nothing I can't handle," Julie replied.

Sarah pointed to the main office windows. Through the glass, the guidance counselors' offices were visible. "We're right here," said Sarah. "Let's make an appointment."

Julie shook her head. "My problems with Lettie and my parents go back a long way. They expect me to be

110

there for her all the time, and I don't have time for myself. I'm glad you and Cindy came over yesterday, but in the long run it doesn't matter. I'm still stuck."

"I'd be glad to keep listening to you," said Sarah. "Hasn't that helped at all?"

Tears welled in Julie's eyes. "Yes. And I really appreciate it." She dug into her pocket and pulled out a tissue. "But it's just not enough."

"On this last worksheet," Mrs. Parisi began, "I want you to be on the lookout for any references to current events. They can be mentions of movies, television programs, sports events like the Super Bowl, or news—even the weather, if it is mentioned." She handed out the worksheets. "Samuel Pepys kept a diary in the seventeenth century in which he gave us his opinions about the Shakespeare plays he saw."

"I bet he didn't do it for a history assignment," Lowell cracked.

"No, but you will," Mrs. Parisi told him.

When the time came to trade diaries, Sarah glanced at Julie. She wasn't exactly surprised when Julie got up to trade with a girl named Carol, but she did feel hurt. Julie had made it clear that she didn't want Sarah intruding in her life any longer. Sarah glanced around the room: Dave had already traded with Jennifer.

Across the room, Julie was having similar problems. Carol already had a partner, too.

"We need someone to trade with Julie," Mrs. Parisi announced. "Sarah?"

There was no way around it. Sarah traded diaries with Julie and returned to her seat. She took a peek at the back pages.

S. and C. came to the house today and gave me and Lettie a perm.

There were no other entries.

After class, Dave could not suppress a smile when Sarah told him that Julie had only added one sentence to her journal. "Aren't you sorry you didn't trade with me before? I've been writing lots."

"It doesn't make sense. She wrote like a fiend before." Sarah riffled through the heavily inked pages. "Can you drop me off at the Madison Arts Guild after school? I want to talk to her after her music lesson."

"Okay, but I can't stick around," he warned. "Mom wanted the car the minute I got out of school."

"That's fine," said Sarah. "This is between Julie and me."

Jennifer arrived at 18 Pine St. that afternoon with the new worksheet and Dave's diary. She headed straight for Kwame. "Here you go," she said, dropping the homework on the table.

Kwame picked up the diary and put it in his backpack. "Did you turn your diary over to Dave?" he asked.

"Yeah," said Jennifer. She pointed to the worksheet. "Would you mind getting started on it tonight? There's a one-day-only sale at Ms. Tique, and—"

"All right," said Kwame. "But I'm not going to do

112

the whole thing for you."

"I know, I know," said Jennifer. "You keep saying that."

Kwame held up his hands. "Just making sure. I've been doing a good job so far, haven't I?" he said cautiously. "You haven't caught any major...uh, spelling mistakes or anything, have you?"

Jennifer gave him a dazzling smile. "You don't make mistakes, Kwame."

Steve and April arrived shortly after Jennifer left. As Steve helped himself to some french fries from Kwame's basket, Kwame told him about Jennifer's visit.

"Did she notice any difference?" asked Steve through a mouthful of french fries.

"Not a thing. But Dave has her diary now, so we have to let him know what's going on."

"No problem," said Steve. "Dave will think it's funny."

April looked from one boy to the other, bewildered. "What are you two talking about?"

"We can't tell you," said Steve, shaking his head.

"Why not?" said April.

"Because you *won't* think it's funny," said Steve.

Fifteen

When Dave dropped Sarah off at the Madison Arts Guild, she went straight for the room where Julie had had her music lesson earlier in the week, and pressed her ear to the door. She didn't hear anyone inside.

"Can I help you?"

Mr. Hannes stood before her, a steaming cup of coffee in his hand. "Are you looking for Julie?" he asked. Sarah nodded. "So am I," he said. "She's never been this late before."

He invited Sarah to wait with him in his office, but after twenty more minutes, it became clear that Julie was not showing up. She did it, Sarah thought; she actually quit her voice lessons.

As Sarah got up to go, Mr. Hannes handed her two photocopied music sheets. "Her lesson for next week, in case you see her before I do," he explained.

On the street, Sarah checked her watch. Julie would not be expected at home for another fifteen minutes. I could go to her house and wait for her, Sarah thought. She knew the baby-sitter would let her in. But Julie had seemed so desperate that morning. Sarah had a strong feeling that Julie would not be going home that day.

Instead, Sarah began to walk toward 18 Pine St. It was twelve blocks away, but she needed the time to think.

When she arrived at the pizza shop, she waved to Kwame, Steve, and April and made her way to the pay phone. She punched in the O'Connors' number.

"Julie, is that you?" asked the baby-sitter at the O'Connor home. Sarah could hear Lettie crying in the background.

"No, I was wondering if Julie was at home," said Sarah.

"She isn't," snapped the baby-sitter. "If she isn't here in five minutes, I'll have to call her mother at work. I have to get back to my own kids."

Sarah hung up and stared at the receiver. Julie had disappeared, as her diary had suggested. She remembered the last time she'd seen Julie that day. It had been at the pay phones at school. Her heart started pounding as she remembered how Julie had hastily

116

rubbed at what she had written on the booth. Who had Julie called? Sarah wondered. It was a faint hope, but maybe Julie hadn't erased what she'd written completely. You don't have anything else to go on, girl, Sarah told herself.

"Steve, I need you to do me a big favor," said Sarah. "Can you drive me back to the school?"

Steve's eyebrows shot up. "Did you forget something?"

"Sort of. I can't tell you why right now, but it's very important. Please?" said Sarah.

"Why won't you tell me what it is?" said Steve.

"Look who's talking!" said April. "You and Kwame have been giggling all afternoon about your secret, and now you want Sarah to tell you hers."

Sarah gave April a grateful smile as Steve put on his coat and headed for the door of the pizza shop.

"Can't you drive any faster?" said Sarah when they were on the way.

Steve pressed on the accelerator, and the battered Toyota whined more loudly. When they got to the school, the driveway was empty, but there were still a few pickup trucks parked around the side. Sarah pulled at the main doors, but they didn't open.

"They're locked," said Steve, shivering slightly. "What happened? Did you leave a book in your locker?"

Sarah pounded on the door with her hand. Steve ran to the side of the building and found a rock.

"You're not going to break the window, are you?"

said Sarah.

"Of course not! But watch." He smacked the rock against the metal beam between the doors, and the noise echoed loudly in the empty building.

"School's out," said the custodian who appeared at the door a few minutes later.

"I need to get a number from that phone booth right there," said Sarah, pointing behind the man. The custodian shook his head and turned away. Sarah grabbed the rock from Steve's hand and pounded on the door again. This time the custodian looked at her angrily.

"This is a matter of life and death!" Sarah shouted. "Let me in."

"Put that rock away," the custodian growled. "You can come in—but make it quick."

Sarah ran to the phone and searched the booth. There were dozens of numbers written on the walls. Sarah closed her eyes and tried to remember where she had seen Julie's hand. At last she located a half-smeared number on the wall: "G. 555-2357."

Sarah dug into her pocketbook and found some change. After dialing the number, she glanced at the custodian, who was busy lecturing Steve about throwing rocks. The phone rang many times before a woman finally answered.

"Greyhound Bus Lines," she said. "How may I help you?"

Sixteen

"Faster, Steve!" Sarah cried.

"I'm driving as fast as I can," Steve said.

Where could Julie be going? Sarah wondered. She thought of the places a runaway usually went. New York City? She imagined Julie walking off a bus alone there, and the thought chilled her. Los Angeles? Julie probably did not have the money for a trip out there. She leafed through Julie's diary for a clue but did not see any cities listed. There were only references to her pressures at home and accounts of Lettie, Rashad, Mr. Hannes, and her brother, Brian.

"Kentucky!" said Sarah out loud.

"What about it?" said Steve.

"Nothing," said Sarah, her heart beating faster. Brian went to a college in Kentucky. Of the entire family, he was the one Julie seemed to feel comfortable around. Sarah's heart began to pound against her chest.

Steve pulled into a parking area reserved for buses to let Sarah out. "You want me to wait for you?" he asked.

Sarah hesitated. The bus station wasn't in a great neighborhood, but she'd better not involve Steve in Julie's problems. The other girl was already mistrustful of Sarah.

"No," said Sarah, "but thanks." They reached the bus station, and Sarah ran out of the car and into the lobby.

Inside the high-ceilinged building, the air smelled faintly of tobacco and diesel fumes. Sarah scanned the nearly empty room for any signs of Julie. She saw an elderly couple watching television on the coin-operated sets. An old man with a grizzled beard had stretched out on a bench near the candy machines.

When she reached the ticket counter, she looked at the Departures sign, but Kentucky was not listed among the buses leaving that day.

"Are there any buses going to Bowling Green, Kentucky, today?" she asked the woman at the counter.

"Not directly. You have to take the one to St. Louis, then transfer. You want a ticket?"

"No, thanks," said Sarah, looking up at the departure time for the St. Louis bus. It left at 5:02. Maybe

Julie will show up before then, Sarah thought. It was 4:15.

She found a pay phone near the snack machines and dialed Julie's house again. A different woman answered, and Sarah guessed it was Julie's mother.

"Is Julie home?" Sarah asked.

"No," said a worried-sounding Mrs. O'Connor. "Is this Sarah Gordon?"

"Yes! How did you know?"

"She doesn't get a lot of phone calls," said Mrs. O'Connor. "And she has been talking about you for two weeks. The fact is, I'm a little angry with you for doing Lettie's hair yesterday. What if you had burned her?"

"Cindy and I were very careful," said Sarah.

"You never know what could have happened," Mrs. O'Connor insisted. Then she sighed. "I'm looking at Lettie now, and I have to admit you two did a beautiful job on her. On both my daughters. Julie isn't with you?"

"No," said Sarah, "but I'm looking for her." She was about to tell Mrs. O'Connor where she suspected Julie was going, but then changed her mind. Sarah wanted to see if she could talk to Julie first.

"You tell her to come straight home if you see her, you hear?" said Mrs. O'Connor angrily.

Sarah promised, then hung up. She used the last quarter she had to dial her house.

"Tasha? It's me. I need your help, girl. I've got some money behind the mirror in my room. Call a cab and

121

come down to the bus station!"

"What's going on?" said Tasha.

"I'll tell you when you get here. Hurry!"

Sarah waited for her cousin at one·of the coin-operated televisions. She'd changed her mind about being alone in the station. If Julie was angry that Tasha was with her, she'd just have to deal with it.

"Hello." A grizzled white man stood in front of her. He wore a pair of cotton pants that were too short in the legs, and a quilted blue jacket. His breath smelled like alcohol.

"I'll leave you alone if you want me to," said the man, not moving. "I was just standing over there and I saw this pretty girl and I thought I'd say hello."

"Hello," said Sarah quickly.

The man smiled. "That's better," he said. "My name is Owen. You going off to visit family?"

"Excuse me, but I'm looking for someone," said Sarah. She tried to catch the eye of the woman behind the counter, to show her that the man was bothering her, but the woman was on the phone.

"Sorry," he said, looking apologetic. "All I did was ask a simple question. It's none of my business where you're going." He moved off.

Sarah watched Owen walk toward the snack area. He reached into the duffel bag of the man who was sleeping on the bench there and pulled out a bottle, which he put to his lips. He caught Sarah looking at him and raised the bottle toward her as if he were making a toast. Sarah looked away quickly.

122

Ten minutes later Tasha arrived. "What's going on?"

Sarah told her about Julie's diary, the mysterious crossed-out message, and the phone number Julie had tried to erase earlier that day.

"What if she doesn't show up here?" asked Tasha. "Is there any other place she could be?"

"I don't know," said Sarah. "I thought about—" She stopped in midsentence. "Uh-oh, here he comes again."

Tasha looked up to see Owen grinning at her. "I see you brought a friend with you," he said, winking at Sarah.

"Excuse me," said Tasha loudly. "This is a private conversation!" The elderly couple sitting nearby looked over, and the ticket vendor looked up from the phone.

"No need to be rude," Owen mumbled.

"Please leave us alone before I call a cop," said Tasha in her loudest voice.

Owen cursed at Tasha before shuffling away.

"Dang, Tasha. He was just a drunk," Sarah murmured.

"Just a drunk?" Tasha echoed. "Drunk people can be dangerous. If you'd lived in Oakland like I did, you wouldn't take chances."

At ten minutes before five, an announcement came over the P.A. system. "Passengers headed for St. Louis and connecting points to Bowling Green, Nashville, and points south, please board at Gate Five."

Sarah and Tasha hurried to the gate outside. There

was only a bit of daylight left, and the streetlights had come on. They saw Julie standing in the line with her ticket out.

"How did she get past us?" cried Tasha, breaking into a run.

"We must have been talking to Owen," Sarah replied. She was running with her bookbag, and Tasha was soon several paces ahead.

Tasha arrived at the line just as Julie was about to hand her ticket to the driver. "Julie, wait!"

"I've made up my mind, Tasha," said Julie. When Sarah arrived, Julie scowled at her. "I see you told your cousin about my problems. And Cindy knows everything, too. Who else knows?"

"No one," said Sarah. "I told Tasha because I had to. You need to talk to someone, too, Julie."

"Are you getting on board, miss?" the bus driver asked.

Without thinking, Sarah grabbed the ticket out of Julie's hand.

"Give that back!" Julie cried.

The bus driver touched a walkie-talkie in his pocket. "Do you want me to call the cops, miss?" he asked Julie.

Sarah looked at Julie pleadingly. "Five minutes, that's all I want. Let's talk for five minutes."

Julie picked up her duffel bag and gave the bus driver a weary look. "Don't call the cops," she said.

Seventeen

"Your problems will be waiting for you when you come back," said Sarah.

The three girls stood next to a water fountain inside the station. Through the window they could see that most of the passengers had boarded the bus already. The bus driver was stowing the last of the luggage in the compartments beneath the seats.

"Who said I was coming back?" said Julie.

"You can't run away for good," said Tasha.

"Easy for you to say," said Julie. "You don't live with my parents." She was quiet for a moment. "If I go home now," she said slowly, "all I'll get is punishment

125

for not baby-sitting Lettie. Nothing will have changed. I can't go back there."

"Who said anything about going home?" said Sarah. "We'll go over to 18 Pine St. and figure something out."

"I did everything I could to make things easy on my parents," said Julie. "I took care of Lettie, I got dinner started, I fixed breakfast for her, I did my homework and all my chores, and they still asked me to do more." Tears brimmed in her eyes. "Don't you see? I gave it my best shot."

"But we didn't give it *our* best shot," said Sarah, pointing to Julie, Tasha, and herself.

The bus driver came over to the window and knocked on the glass. "The bus is leaving," he mouthed.

Sarah and Tasha held their breath as Julie ran toward the driver. When she returned to them, she picked up her bags and headed for the ticket window. "He said I can cash in the ticket and get my money back."

Mr. Harris waved to Sarah and Tasha as they walked into the pizzeria. The Gordon cousins led Julie to their booth in the back of the shop.

"I talked to your mom on the phone this afternoon," said Sarah. "She was mad at me for giving Lettie the perm yesterday. She said I could have burned her."

"She yelled at me, too," said Julie. "I didn't want to put that in the diary, so I didn't write much for our last assignment."

"I noticed," said Sarah.

"Speaking of parents, maybe you should call yours to let them know you're all right," said Tasha. Julie made a sour face at the suggestion but walked to the pay phone.

"Come with me," Julie told Sarah. "I'm going to need your moral support."

As soon as Julie said, "Hello, Mom," Sarah could hear Mrs. O'Connor beginning to yell at her. "I'm all right, Mom," Julie went on. "I'll be coming home soon—No, don't put him on.... Hi, Dad...I'm fine.... I'm at 18 Pine St. It's a pizza shop. Wait, Daddy!"

Julie hung up the phone in defeat. "He's on his way over," she said. Tasha joined them at the phone booth, and Julie recounted their conversation. "I should have gotten on that bus." She wrinkled her brow in thought. "Sarah, how did you know I was going to Kentucky?"

"I had to play detective," said Sarah. "I went back to Murphy to read that number you wrote on the wall at lunch this morning."

"Nice going," said Tasha admiringly.

"How come you didn't show up at the bus station until the last minute?"

Julie squirmed. "There was this creepy drunk guy who kept coming on to me at the station."

"Owen!" cried Sarah.

Julie laughed. "I didn't get his name. He kept wanting to talk to me, so I went to a diner across the street

127

and waited there."

"Good thinking. Do you think your parents could get another baby-sitter to stay with Lettie for a longer period after school?" said Sarah, getting back to the problem.

"Maybe," said Julie. "But I...uh, don't have many friends, so I usually went home anyway. Since I was at home, they figured they didn't need a baby-sitter. But it's one thing to go home on your own; it's another to be forced to go home every single day."

"Tell them that!" Sarah and Tasha chorused.

While they waited for Mr. O'Connor to arrive, Sarah remembered the sheet music Mr. Hannes had given her. She was handing it to Julie when Mr. Harris arrived at the booth with three slices of pizza.

"On the house," he said. "I'm trying a new tomato sauce recipe and I need your opinions." He waited with arms folded as Tasha and Sarah tasted it. At first Julie politely refused, but Mr. Harris would have none of it. "Take a big bite," he ordered.

"It's wonderful," said Julie through the mouthful. She looked at Tasha and Sarah, who were shaking their heads.

"I like the old one better," said Tasha. Sarah agreed. "Trust me, you'd like the old one better, too," Tasha told Julie.

"That's what everybody tells me." Mr. Harris sighed. "I thought I had a winner there."

As Mr. Harris was walking away, Julie pointed to his shoe. On the sole was a piece of pepperoni

128

smashed flat against the heel. The sight of it popping into view as he walked back to the counter struck them as funny, and they collapsed into fits of laughter. What made Sarah even happier was the way Julie attacked her slice of pizza. And the rest of Sarah's.

"Here he is," said Julie suddenly. The Gordon cousins turned to find Mr. O'Connor, a nearly bald man with a thick mustache, scanning the room for his daughter.

"Tell them what you told us," Sarah whispered. Julie was getting nervous. Her father had spotted her and was walking toward them, his mouth a firm angry line.

"They won't listen," Julie whispered.

Sarah suddenly reached into her backpack. She pulled out Julie's diary and placed it in the other girl's hands. "Maybe they'll listen to this."

Eighteen

It was almost seven o'clock when the Gordon cousins finally got home. Mr. Gordon was upset about their missing dinner, but his scowl faded when Sarah and Tasha offered to finish cleaning the kitchen for him.

Sarah was glad to see Allison and Pam watching television together. The two friends had obviously made up.

"Allison, can I see you a minute?" Sarah asked. Allison hit the Pause button on the VCR and followed Sarah out of the room.

"What happened to Vaughn?" Sarah whispered.

"We broke up," Allison said matter-of-factly. "Pam

131

was right—he was boring."

Sarah returned to the kitchen, shaking her head.

"I heard everything," Tasha said.

"If she's like this now," said Sarah, "what's she going to be like when she's sixteen?"

Tasha laughed. "I'm wondering what she'll be like when she's *thirteen*!"

On Friday José arrived at the cafeteria and dropped his bookbag in the middle of the table with a loud thump. Everyone, including Julie, looked at him. "Mission accomplished!" he declared. "Sort of."

"You got rid of all the kittens?" said Steve. "I told you that computer bulletin board would get results."

"One guy called me from that system," said José. "My brother found a home for the second one."

"I thought you had three left to give away," said Kwame, looking up from his food.

"That's the interesting part," said José. "My mom noticed that Reina was acting really weird the last few days. Every time we gave away another one of her kittens, she would start yowling and doing you-know-what on the floor. Two days ago, we were down to the last one, and Reina stopped eating and drinking."

"Of course!" cried April. "You were getting rid of her children."

"That's what my mom figured," said José. "Last night Reina and the kitten disappeared. We finally found them in a closet. Reina was grooming the kitten, licking him all over. For the rest of the night, she didn't let him out of her sight."

"Awwww, that's so sad!" cried Jennifer. "You didn't get rid of the last one, did you?"

José shook his head: "There was no way we could separate those two. Starting next week, we'll have two family cats."

"Why next week? Where are they now?" said Tasha.

"They're at home, but next week Reina gets spayed. Until she can stay out of trouble, she and her son are not family cats; they're José's cats!"

Sarah stole a look at Julie O'Connor, who was laughing along with everyone else. That morning, Sarah had opened her locker and found a note from Julie.

Dear Sarah,

Things were a little rough when Dad picked me up from 18 Pine. He lectured me all the way home about my responsibilities. I got more from Mom until Lettie got upset and told them to stop picking on me. For some reason, that really got to my mother.

Mom and Dad read the diary that same night, and they got me out of my room to discuss it. We sat in the kitchen and ate grapes and talked for over an hour. I cried a lot. I couldn't help it!

We can't afford a baby-sitter for Lettie every day, but Dad said if we make some changes, we can have someone at home on the two days I have my voice lessons, so I don't have to run straight home afterward. It's not perfect, but it's better than it was, and it

wouldn't have happened without you. I also wanted
you to know that my parents are making me go talk to
one of the guidance counselors at school. They think I
have some kind of eating disorder. I'm not so sure
about that, but I couldn't argue—not when they just
made all these arrangements for me. Anyway, we'll see
what happens.

Thanks again. You're a great friend.
Julie

Sarah felt Julie nudging her shoulder. "He's cute," Julie whispered, pointing to José.

"He is," Sarah agreed. "Do you want to go after him, or hold out for Rashad?" She smiled at the startled look on Julie's face.

Julie grinned. "And here I thought I was being slick using just his initial," she said. "The problem is, Rashad doesn't know I exist."

"We can change that," said Cindy, who had been listening to them.

Tasha leaned in from the other side. "By the time we do your nails, your makeup, and your wardrobe, you'll be beating back the boys with a stick."

"If that ever happens," Julie assured them, "I'll throw away the stick!"

PINE

Nineteen

In history class that afternoon, Mrs. Parisi took a moment to talk about the diary project. "On the whole, I thought it went very well, although some people took it more seriously than others." She sent a meaningful look in Lowell's direction.

"Since it's Friday," Mrs. Parisi continued, "I thought it would be fun to read a few passages from one of the best diaries. I was quite surprised by the effort this person put into it, but of course I can't say who it is."

Sarah looked at Julie. It's going to be hers, she thought, or mine. She recalled her own diary and the many passages she was proud of.

Mrs. Parisi began to read: *Dear Diary. What a great day I had at the mall! First I went to the salon to get my nails wrapped. It cost seventy dollars, but they look gorgeous. Too bad no one will see my toenails unless I wear sandals.*

Everyone laughed.

I took my charge card with me and bought sixteen sweaters, twelve pairs of slacks, and three more charge cards! Then the store gave me an award for being the two millionth customer. It was very exciting. Afterwards I met my dream man at the video arcade. We kissed for hours next to the Action Bongo machine. He may be a nerdy-looking, music-loving, pizza-addicted history genius, but he's the only one for me.

The class laughed again. There were very few nerdy-looking, music loving, pizza-addicted history geniuses at Murphy High, and everyone knew it was Kwame. Most everyone also knew that Jennifer had conned Kwame into doing her work.

We went to the movies later on. It was a horror movie about a girl who only had a hundred outfits.

Mrs. Parisi chuckled as the class roared. "Here was someone who really had fun with the assignment," she said.

The teacher read another example, and Sarah glanced at Jennifer, who seemed to be frozen in place. Her pretty features were set in an angry scowl. Her eyes were fixed straight ahead. She was so still, Sarah began to get worried.

"Are you okay?" Sarah whispered as the class

136

roared again.

"I'll kill him," Jennifer whispered back. "I'll kill him!"

Coming in Book 12, Taking Sides

"I don't ever want to talk to you again, you racist pig!" Tasha was practically screaming at Rick. The lunchroom got strangely quiet, and everyone was looking at them.

Rick stood up. "What are you talking about, girl?" he asked in a quiet voice.

"I heard about that joke you told. We don't need racists here," said Tasha. She was as upset as Sarah had ever seen her. "Last Friday in the lunch room. You told a stupid joke about Santa Claus."

Rick looked puzzled as he stared at Tasha. "C'mon, Tasha. Marc Halle was there. He's black and he wasn't upset."

"Marc doesn't speak for me or anyone else," stated Tasha. "I want a formal apology, to me and to anyone else who was offended."

When Tasha hears about a racist joke making the rounds at Murphy High, she challenges Rick to a debate. The gang at 18 Pine is split on the issue. Will Tasha get Rick thrown out of school? And will the controversy divide the friends for good?

CHOOSE YOUR OWN ADVENTURE®

Horror–Mystery–Science Fiction–Sports
There are so many adventures to choose from!